As a Child

Corey Mesler

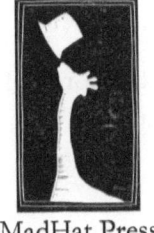

MadHat Press
Asheville, North Carolina

MadHat Press
MadHat Incorporated
PO Box 8364, Asheville, NC 28814

The Library of Congress has assigned
this edition a Control Number of
2014915661

ISBN 978-1-941196-07-6 (paperback)

Text by Corey Mesler
Cover art by Tim Crowder
Book and cover design by MadHat Press

www.madhat-press.com

ADDITIONAL PRAISE FOR *AS A CHILD*

"In *As a Child: Stories*, Corey Mesler is once again tender, inventive, and gently fearless. Mesler's stories transport the reader to a land where nothing matters but the madly beating heart. Be prepared for what you never knew you knew, and hold on tight. It is all there."

—Meg Pokrass, author of *Damn Sure Right*

"Reading the stories in Corey Mesler's marvelous new collection, *As A Child*, I try to figure out how he can so nimbly distill pathos into joy, fear and desire into sweet hilarity, and language itself into a vehicle of pure delight. Magic is the only explanation that comes to mind."

—Steve Stern, author of *The Book of Mischief*

"Corey Mesler has unhinged my brain and filled it with words so artfully arranged that they make me want to weep with envy. He blurs the lines between prose and song so that the writer becomes the singer: observant, lyrical, and passionate. Every story in *As a Child* is a treat."

—Laura Benedict, author of *Bliss House*

ADDITIONAL PRAISE FOR COREY MESLER

"Mesler is one of the unique truly voices of our time...like a slide-guitar Browning, he addresses the reader personally, and you will listen. I find myself getting lost in the metaphors, at first deceptively simple, but in the end profound...and true."
                    —Ward Abel, author of *American Bruise*

"Mesler's poetry is the sky."
                    —Cassie Premo Steele, author of *Ruin*

"Corey Mesler is Broadway Danny Rose. He's Miles Davis. And George Gervin. He's a pro's pro and I love what he does."
                    —Ben Tanzer, author of *Lucky Man*

"The radicality (I know, there's no such word) of Corey Mesler's poetry is its presentation of the terrific values in pieces of being, in protracted moments of verbal attention, in images that make even the awful and perilous things we know—enlightening."
                    —Gordon Osing , author of *Slaughtering the Buddha*

"Corey Mesler is a Memphis treasure— a gaudily gifted poet-fabulist, he's our master of the surreal lyric, our River City Rimbaud, the Charles Simic of the Southland. His poems have wit and soul and refuse to play by any rules save their own."
                    —Bobby Rogers, author of *Paper Anniversary*

"Whether he's reporting from the bowels of the Piggly Wiggly or the capacious birthing canal of an alien on the planet Sniff, the lambent haecceity of Corey Mesler never fails to shine through time and space and the sulfurous stench of the human heart."
                    —Linda Heck, singer-songwriter of *Transformed*

CONTENTS

"Strange angels, desires. Come from beyond us, inhabit our machines."
—John Updike

*"Fear? Of course he feared. Why wouldn't he?/God with all those stars
and stallions!/He with little children's bones."*
—Archibald MacLeish

"Unquenchable desire is finally given its rope: movement begins."
—Joseph Campbell

for Toby and Chloe, children of the long song

PILKIE INVENTS A WORD

"For the work of the pen let the writer be sent a beautiful girl."
—anonymous inscription in 12th c. Latin Bible

When Jerome Pilkie was young his father told him that real money was to be made in inventing, in creating something out of nothing.

"Patents, son," he said, his gin-blossomed face serious and parental. "Think of the man who came up with the paper clip. A simple twist of metal that meant millions to him. Millions!"

Jerome didn't ask his dad why they lived on Morrow Street in a particularly bleak part of Memphis. His father was a butcher and a drunk.

Yet the advice took root.

All through his teen years Jerome Pilkie kept a journal in which he wrote down dozens of ideas, which were either (a) impractical, (b) already invented, or (c) downright fatuous. But it never left his mind that he was destined to create something that had never before existed.

Jerome also had another virtually furtive vice. He was a reader of novels. Good novels, bad novels; it didn't matter, as long as he could live for a while in a fictitious place. So naturally, he was a bit moony. It was while he was reading *Just William* by Richmal Crompton that the brainstorm hit him which would transform his workaday existence into something grand, something heroic, something inspired and transcendent.

Jerome Pilkie was going to invent a word.

It would be his alone, and it would be recorded that before him the word did not exist.

How to start? Pilkie pondered. He owned an unabridged dictionary, of course, so he could make sure that he hadn't been trumped before he even began.

The utilitarian method? The word had to fit and be useful and name something formerly unnamed?

The blind-faith method? Pull some letters from the unconscious, shake them up and see what happened?

The poetic method? Make a word that sounded appealing, like *mumpsimus* or *birdlime*?

The "just connect" method? Make a word that seemed to naturally follow a sequence of already-established words?

The viral method? Put anything together with any definition, put it out there and see if it, like chum, draws word sharks?

Long into his mulish midnights, Pilkie worked with the 26 letters of the Latin-derived alphabet. His method did not consist of simply combining letters into a billion variations. It was a divine alchemy Pilkie was trailing. He knew not where he was heading, but he was confident that he would get there and know the place as his alone. He slept little. He ate only bits of bread and cheese left out on the sideboard.

Pilkie's boss at the stationery store stopped calling after a week and sent him a letter of dismissal which Pilkie never read. He also never opened any of his bills received during this time. The mail piled up. The newspapers piled up. The neighbors debated about calling the police. "He was always an odd duck," they prepared in advance of the "shocking" revelations, whatever they may be. They longed for figures of authority to appear.

Pilkie worked at this feverish pace for 21 days, at the end of which he collapsed at his desk. A swoon of sleep overtook him.

He woke 28 hours later, his head full of floss, his eyes crusted over, his body rank. He was stiff and stood tentatively, bones cracking. He shuffled like an automaton to his living room window and opened the drapes. The sunlight went through his head like a song made of glass.

Who am I? Pilkie thought. The answer *Jerome Pilkie* did not satisfy. *What am I?* he asked further.

A man. A searcher. A utopian. A fool.

He walked to his desk with failure hanging from him like crepe. The room resembled a prisoner's garret. He was tired, tired. His escritoire was a shambles. There on the desk, amid crumbs of dried crust and hard cheese, lay his worksheets, the topmost stained with saliva where he had slavered in his slumber.

He picked up the soiled sheet and read what he had written there.

He shook his head and read it again.

About halfway down the paper, after various doodles and scrawls and crossed-out alphabetiforms, half-obscured by his blob of leaky spittle, was a combination of letters that Pilkie did not remember putting together. He gingerly wiped the drool spot away so as not to smear his results.

Jesus, Pilkie said to himself. Holy Mother of God. Did I write this?

Pilkie moved to the couch, turned on the nearby floor lamp, sheet in hand. He sat and read it over a number of times. His neck tickled. His thumbs pricked. Holy Mother of God, he repeated. This is it.

Jerome Pilkie had created his new word.

Pilkie took a hot bath. He found a steak in his freezer and grilled it in a frying pan along with some instant potatoes and baby green peas. He made coffee conscientiously, treating himself to a rich brew. He ate alone at his dining room table, his head awhirl with new planets, himself the sun. In his mind he was tasting success, the first of his life, and it felt heady. It was the most important thing he'd ever done. He must now be careful. He felt himself on the brink of great good fortune, and the fall from such optimism could kill.

He dressed with care. He put a single sheet of foolscap into the typewriter and carefully typed out the few letters that were his new word, and after it a concise definition.

Then he called his friend, Mike, who was a writer. Briefly he described to Mike what he had done, without actually telling him the new word.

"Jeez, Pilkie," Mike said. "I don't know, you know? Are you okay? I've called a dozen times."

"Fine, fine," Pilkie said. "Please, the word. What do I do next?"

Mike exhaled. "I'll call my agent. Maybe he'll know."

"Thank you, Mike," Pilkie said and hung up.

A few days went by. Pilkie had almost talked himself into another route, bypassing Mike's agent. Perhaps he should go straight to a copyright lawyer, or perhaps the Library of Congress.

Finally, Mike's agent, Gilberte Sans, called. She had a voice like the mother in a TV sitcom.

"Jerome," she began. "May I call you Jerome?"

"Yes, yes," Jerome said, impatiently.

"Mike told me your—ahem, discovery."

"I didn't discover it. It's not like the Pacific Ocean. It never existed before me."

"Of course," Gilberte Sans said. "Would you tell me the word?"

"Absolutely not," Pilkie said.

"Okay." Gilberte Sans paused. "Fair enough. Can you come into the office and I'll get our lawyer to meet with us? Say tomorrow at 11?"

"Can't it be today?"

On the other end of the phone Pilkie heard breathing, either in exasperation or perplexity.

"I could move some things around, I suppose."

The meeting was set for 2 p.m. that afternoon.

Jerome Pilkie arrived at the office dressed in his best suit. Under his arm was an envelope. Inside the envelope was the single sheet of paper containing his word and its definition.

Once in the office, Pilkie began to get nervous. It was all so weighty and official looking. The secretary smiled at Jerome and asked him to have a seat.

Finally he was shown into Gilberte Sans' office. She stood and extended her hand. Gilberte Sans was the most beautiful woman Pilkie had ever seen. She was almost six feet tall and her hair was the color of loam. Her cheekbones were wings. Her hand, when Pilkie grasped it, was as warm as breast milk.

The other person in the room was a small bald man. He was about the size of a broom.

"Grif," the bald man said.

It might as well have been a dog's bark. Pilkie could not take his eyes off Gilberte Sans.

"Sit, please," the siren spoke.

Somehow Pilkie lined up his rear over a chair and sat.

Pilkie imagined that the envelope in his lap was about to make a break for it, muscle the window open and fly away.

After some preliminary talk about what led them all to this meeting the lawyer spoke.

"Mr. Pilkie, although this is unprecedented, I believe we can try to accommodate your desires, if I understand them correctly."

Pilkie was growing uncomfortable. Was he crazy? Was he doing the right thing? What if they fleeced him?

They did not fleece him. They drew up a contract that very afternoon. At the bottom of the contract, as if at the mystical consummation at the end of a pact, Jerome Pilkie wrote down his word and its definition.

Now, he thought. *Now, I am sending my child out to the world. Now, this word goes forth and becomes whatever it will become, part of the world's syllabary, part of advertisements or handbills, dissertations or epic poems, journalism or the next* War and Peace. *Jerome Pilkie's word, the one he gave to mankind.* Pilkie allowed himself some hopeful daydreams.

It is well known what happened next. Pilkie's word did indeed make a splash and that splash made Pilkie sopping rich. Coca-Cola alone paid him millions for its use. An obscure poet in Goodland, Kansas paid him $100. Pilkie was open to every negotiation, large or small. He gave the word gratis to Memphis poet John Reed, because, Pilkie reasoned, Memphis artists look out for each other.

And Pilkie's patented word did indeed make its way into one of the crowning achievements of late 20th-century American fiction. You know the author and his magnum opus, *On to Rio Boho*, which used the word 127 times. At the time of this writing it is still on the bestseller list.

Jerome Pilkie and Gilberte Sans were married and moved into a Beaux Arts villa in the South of France. Their personal library is said to exceed 25,000 volumes; everything from Proust to *Just William*. Pilkie's word was translated first into French and then into all the Romance languages and is, as we speak, being converted into Farsi, Arabic, Chinese, Hindi, Finnish and Twi.

You know the word and you may even use it daily. Do not write it down, of course, or attempt in any way to make a profit from it. Pilkies' team of lawyers will be all over you like a tempest after a flame.

The Pilkies, Jerome and Gilberte, raised three children, two boys and a girl. The oldest son, Gulley, was often in trouble with the law, though he had a good heart and a sweet disposition. He looked like a young Mickey Rooney, with a cowlick that seemed defiant. After the third time Pilkie was called to the police station, he took Gulley aside and spoke to him, man to man.

The boy hung his contrite head yet his eyes sparkled with chicanery.

"Gulley," he said. "Find your way. You have your own destiny. You're going to have to have faith in what I am saying now. Listen to this part carefully. The world is not yet full— not by half—and there will be room and time for you to make something out of nothing, something all your own, something only Gulley Pilkie could have made. And making something out of nothing is—ah, son—Man's most honored and exalted aspiration."

A VERY SHORT STORY ABOUT A HIRED GUN

Jack woke up in a strange bed in a strange country. Beside him was a blonde, her back as smooth as a billow. Jack checked the bedside table; his piece was still loaded. There was a mirror on the wall next to the bed and Jack eased out from under the covers to have a look at himself. A stranger stared back. It was almost as if he were in disguise, but that was another country, another blonde. Jack stared until his focus blurred. He wondered if he should wake her up. He needed some tomato juice and maybe another fuck. He needed to be put to rights again. Jack was a little hazy about who he was, where he was, and if, somehow, there was a private place where he was needed.

DANTE GATOR

Burke Tallage was a Dante Gator fan, a real Dante Gator fan. You know Dante's mid-career output, from *Cock-a-Hoop* to *Scrawl* to *Cloudmountaincalling*, the albums that brought the inevitable Dylan comparisons down upon his young head. But Burke knew it all. He knew the whole story as if he had written it. He had followed Dante's career from the first crude basement recordings with his teenage band, Snit Pitchers, to his first public show at the Goner Records Fest, and on to the national stage, from whence Dante became the famous but reclusive genius of the post-rock circuit. *Post-rock,* they called it, because all the old names had been used up.

Burke Tallage was Memphis. He was Memphis the way Big Star was, or Shelby Foote, or Bill Eggleston. Except that Burke was more a moon than a star. He lived off reflected light. Among the Memphis cognoscenti, especially the musically hip cognoscenti—that is, those who wore their nimbi as if they were porkpie hats—Burke was one of the hipper cats. He was known in these circles as the first guy to any gig, the first one to discover new bands, the first to declare when a star's star had reached its apex and was now hurtling toward predestined burnout. And Burke was the first and foremost Dante Gator fan.

Some said Burke discovered Dante, but that would imply that he somehow pushed his career forward, somehow was responsible for the meteoric rise of the singer/songwriter. This is not true. Dante Gator was hoisted on his own petard, so to speak, if a petard can be unearthly guitar skills and a way with words that his namesake would envy. Maybe that's overstating the case. But Dante's lyrics certainly were the envy of his generation, meatier than Milk Mabry's, more cutting than Levi Pangborn's, certainly more memorable than either of the songwriters for Neurotic Dorks with New Clothes, or Chism. Dante wrote from deep wellsprings. His voice, both on the page and in the studio, was a thing to behold, a twister, a temblor, a natural force.

Ironically, it was Dante Gator's reworking of the standard, "Gallows Pole," which first broke him nationally. His version, with its Aeolian harp and haunting backwards background singers, owed nothing to Led Zeppelin's, though that battle continues to this day on the internet, Zep fans notoriously loyal and always spoiling for a fight in defense of their rock-god heroes. This is as it should be. Nevertheless, Gator's version went to number two, an amazing feat for a first-time record, and, if not for Snotgun's "Some New Meanings from Weather," he would have gone straight to number one. He was suddenly the hottest new voice in music.

From there Gator proceeded to manufacture both hits and critically acclaimed CDs, culminating in 2001's *Fifth Watch Bells*, which contained his biggest hit to date, the plaintive "Gayla in the Morning." It was "Gayla" that he sang at the Concert for Climate Control. It was "Gayla" that was covered by everyone from Bad Plus (their de-constructed instrumental version one of Dante's favorite covers of his work) to Doug Hoekstra to The

Art Kane Jazz Mouths. It was "Gayla" that won the Grammy, and, when it was later used in the film *Spondulicks*, the Oscar. Quite a trip for one little song.

And most folks agree that it was the success of "Gayla" that drove Dante Gator underground. Not that he was not already aloof, sequestered, solitary. He shied from the spotlight almost immediately it was shone on him. Yet his reputation still swelled like a cake rising. And after "Gayla" he all but disappeared, except, that is, to materialize every 10–14 months in a studio with an A-list of musicians to record his latest opus. This, in brief, is the story of Dante Gator. Where he is at any given time is anyone's guess. Attempts, over the years, to locate him for interviews or awards, have proven fruitless. He once issued a terse press release. It said: *All I have to say is in my songs.*

But, let's backtrack a little, back to Memphis and Burke's reputation as the principal Dante Gator devotee, the authority both locally and, after he was interviewed by both *Rolling Stone* and *Rock Paper* (it was critic Shlomo Shearsman, who, in *Rock Paper*, called Gator's music "post-rock"), nationally. Burke Tallage was to Dante Gator what George Klein was to Elvis, you know, Presley. From the time of Gator's first appearance at the Goner Fest, introduced by Eric as "the next big thing from Memphis," Burke was the singer/songwriter's shadow, traveling with him from gig to gig, sometimes carrying equipment, sometimes carrying a laptop on which he kept track of all Gator's appearances, sometimes carrying the cliché stash. Burke was something between a roadie and an unofficial manager. Mostly, he was just always there, on the scene, macking the groupies, hanging with the other musicians and their wives (especially Joan Self Selvidge, but that's another story), getting his share of drugs and women. He was a rock star without making any music. It was a heady time for Burke and he readily admitted it. "I have been made by my enthusiasm for and commitment to Dante Gator, and that is all right with me," he told *The Lamplighter*, Memphis' hip Midtown neighborhood newspaper.

Now, at this time, Burke had a day job. Though it was said that Dante was generous with his earnings and kept Burke paid up for his aiding and abetting, Burke managed to also eke out a living with his employment at Cat's Music. There he was an out-front guy, a salesman who could tell you who played on which Mudboy and the Neutrons CD, which Little Big Town was their best, what was the connective link between The Monkees and Captain Beefheart, what famous '60s burnout released a CD under the pseudonym Dark Moon Lilith, and whether Ghostface Killah peaked with *Fishscale*. He knew his music, Burke did.

But, mostly, Burke was renowned for regaling any customer who would listen with tales from the Book of Dante Gator. He spread the gospel of Gator. Sometimes, but rarely, a customer could be seen sidling away from the harangue. But Burke's passion was most often infectious and it is incalculable how many copies of *Cock-a-Hoop* or *Scrawl* or *Bethlehem Holiday Inn* he sold with his romances. Cat's was right happy to have him.

Then something went wrong. There are as many conflicting versions of the story as there are storytellers. Something went wrong between Burke and Dante. The aforementioned Ms. Selvidge told it this way: "Something went wrong between Burke and Dante. Dante, infamously prickly about his private time, seemed to think Burke was *too present*. Too into him. At one live gig—I think it was at Otherlands—Dante said from the stage, 'Burke Tallage is here tonight, ladies and gentlemen, to update my address book and lick up my spilt milk. Burke, take a bow, you suck-up sycophant.' The expression on Burke's face was something to behold. It was like a cross between a hurt puppy and that kid in *The Omen*. Later—and God knows why Burke stayed with him after this—Dante accused him of hitting on his girlfriend of the time, the famous Memphis siren Amy Fayaway. Amy's story, alone, could fill a book, and her time with Dante was the stuff of local legend. She was all legs and hair and hunger. I say this with all love and respect. She was a harpy. And Dante was crazy about her. I doubt Burke could even get in her door, so to speak, but you never know. She was a disreputable pinkpants."

Another version has them falling out over money but this seems unlikely. As previously mentioned, Dante Gator was generous. He was generous, mainly because he didn't really care about money. He didn't care about fame. He only wanted to work, to write songs. And, some said, he only recorded his own songs because he thought no one else could do them justice. Otherwise he would have been happy just writing them, selling them, letting them go like Noah's enthusiastic birds.

Still, another version of the falling-out was that Burke eventually, for his efforts, wanted to actually get credit on Dante's recordings. Now, it must be said, that Dante should have at least included a thank-you to his number one fan on at least one of the CDs, but he didn't. For whatever reason, he didn't. But Burke, you understand, wanted a recording credit, a background singer credit, something, anything. He began to see his life slipping away. He began to sense that moon-quality aforesaid. This perhaps began to rankle after that ill-famed Otherlands gig. Burke Tallage, for all his love for Dante Gator, still wanted to be an individual, still wanted to be his own man. He had his pride.

Eric from Goner had this to say: "I was there one night when Dante locked Burke out. Literally, locked him out of his trailer, that rattle-trap behemoth that they traveled in for a while. He left Burke standing in the rain outside Brownville, Tennessee, with no way to get home but his thumb. It was not very nice, but, then I don't know what precipitated it. I don't know what Burke, you know, had done."

Burke Tallage walked home that night. He walked all the way from Brownsville in the rain. And when he got home he holed up in his apartment, with a high-quality case of pneumonia, and he refused to see anyone. Fearing another Johnny Eatman tragedy (Johnny "Singer" died, you remember, from the flu, alone in his apartment, during the cold winter holidays) some friends dropped by and attempted to kick their way inside. They got an earful for their efforts. But, at least, they left assured that Burke was still alive; alive and very very angry.

Burke took a turn for the worse then. Some said he left town for a while, lived in St. Louis with a leggy writer for *St. Louis Magazine*, where his drinking first began to seem dangerous. Some said he never left town, just took to his room and drank himself into a livid daze every night. Whatever happened during those months and months of wandering in the desert, by the time Burke reappeared Dante Gator had already moved on, first relocating to Nashville and then from there to the fame and fortune iterated above. And when Dante went under, when he disappeared from the public radar and only emerged to record, ironically Burke was remaking himself yet again. It was around this time that Burke picked up an acoustic guitar and tried to make it as a punk folkie, using Neil Young, the way so many had before him, as a template.

Burke's "career" was short-lived. He recorded one song, a song that had some local airplay on WEVL, a song later covered by Two Way Radio, the ballad "Thanksgiving on the 13th Floor." He played a couple times in support of Rob Junglkas at Otherlands, a couple times opened for Lucero at The Hi-Tone. He even, briefly, joined Old People Falling, that loose conglom of Memphis music mojo that also included, at one time or another, the Dickinson boys, a few ex-Hellcats, Greg Cartwright, Alicja Trout, Ross Johnson and on and on. But Burke was, by all reports, a dreadful singer and a worse songwriter. He soon returned to his exile, and to his paramount ally, the bottle. It was sad. Many folks tried to help Burke Tallage return from the darkness, Memphians being notably supportive of their own, and many had to shrug and walk away before they themselves were pulled into the whirlpool of his self-destruction. Sad it was.

The news of Dante Gator's first televised performance in a decade was greeted with equal amounts skepticism and joy. This was after years of being an eremite. A press release emerged from somewhere. It said, simply, *Dante Gator will premiere his new song, "What is Deepak Chopra?" on the David Letterman Show.* Stay tuned. No date was announced which led some to speculate that it was a jape, possibly emanating from Dante himself.

But a jape it was not. Soon more concrete details emerged. On September 27th. His only fellow guest was going to be Bob Dylan himself, playing behind Dante. Letterman had at first balked at such demands but recognized, quickly enough, the enormous publicity that this would engender. His ratings would soar.

As the date approached folks in Memphis buzzed with pride and, as usual, some insouciant, hipster jadedness. "Cool," was the usual response when asked if you had heard. "Will you be watching?" was asked as often as "Can the Tigers go to #1?" Some parties were organized around the airing. The Hi-Tone was offering a special night of open mike, followed by a big-screen showing of the broadcast. The hype around this re-emergence was remarkable. It was as if J. D. Salinger had decided it was time to publish another novel.

That night, on TVs across America, a significant thing happened. At the prescribed hour for the David Letterman show to begin a message ran across the screen. "The previously scheduled appearance by Dante Gator and Bob Dylan has been cancelled. A rerun of a previously aired David Letterman show will take its place." A rerun? No Dante Gator?

Some in Memphis sniffed their superiority. There was an I-told-you-so hanging in the air. Dante Gator had goofed America. This was punk theater. This was rock's ornery side, its stubborn refusal to conform. Theories instantly began to spread like a contagion.

The devastating truth would come out by morning. And this is the version most of us know.

The afternoon of the broadcast, when the show is taped in front of a live audience, it was rainy and cold in New York City. The backdoor of NBC studios was barely discernible in the downpour. There was the customary swarm of autograph seekers, perhaps slightly larger than usual, huddled together like geese. Every car that entered that space was met with a throng, surrounded the way an oil spill surrounds sea life. Finally, *the* limousine arrived, pulling up like some dream vehicle, laggardly like a hearse. There was some jostling for position, some reporters and photographers using their practiced wiles to elbow closer. When the door of the limo was opened by the beefy driver the small figure that emerged could have been Dylan or Dante. No one had seen Dante for years and, in the rain, in the murk of Mid-Manhattan mist, who knew?

One man in the crowd knew. One man recognized him. He should—he had followed him practically from his infancy. Burke Tallage stepped forward like an emissary from another planet. His extended hand could have held a keepsake or a rose.

Burke spoke in an undertone. "Hello, Dante," he said. And as Dante raised his cowled face he saw that what was proffered was neither keepsake nor rose. It was a small, chromium-plated pistol. The report was almost swallowed by the noise of the crowd rushing forward. Few saw Dante Gator fall. He was caught by the driver and Bob Dylan, who stepped from the car just as the shot rang out. Someone in the crowd grabbed Burke Tallage, who smiled as if his life had come full circle in that very moment. He smiled because he knew it was all over. Whatever it was, it was all over.

The death of Dante Gator dominated the news for days. The life of Burke Tallage, now called Burke Myshkin Tallage, was quickly cobbled together for CNN and E Channel fare. It was the John Lennon story all over again, was the tack of most reports. A deranged fan. A man haunted by his own demons, his own failed ambitions. Few outside Memphis knew the story, of course, not that it mattered. Dante Gator was dead. And Burke Tallage was in jail for the rest of his life.

So it briefly seemed.

Then, outside the New York City Centre Street Jail, known affectionately as The Tombs, Burke Tallage met his Jack Ruby. Some later blamed the police for their nonchalant protection. But, who saw this coming? Her name was Vivien Cecilia Valerian. Her weapon was a small-caliber pistol, whose bang sounded more like a whimper. Her greeting was simple: "Hello, Burke." She was, according to her diary, Dante Gator's #1 fan.

That Burke Tallage died of such a small hole in his epidermis was an unlucky circumstance. Again, there was blame placed on the authorities, who didn't get him to a hospital quickly enough. He did bleed an extraordinary amount. A doctor could tell you what vital interior plumbing the mini-ball had punctured. Whatever it was, whatever it did, Burke Tallage bled to death before he ever reached the emergency room. He was as dead as Dante Gator, as dead as Elvis. You know; Presley.

Back in Memphis the bad news spread among the Midtown habitués of clubs and record shops. Much insider murmuring, much hand-wringing, much personal guilt, as if any of this could have been prevented. The funerals of their two fallen sons were only a few days apart. Dante Gator's memorial service was a must-attend, see-and-be-seen event. Some people still talk about Jim Dickinson's eulogy for his fallen comrade, orated in that Mississippi growl that many are familiar with. There wasn't a dry eye, as they say, in the crowd; a crowd, by some estimates, that reached 10,000 mourners. Amy Fayaway, even though medicated, had to be carried away from the casket, as she tried to climb inside. This all on a balmy, bright Tuesday afternoon, one of those rare fall days Memphis serves up to remind you why you live in the South rather than, say, North Dakota. Everyone who is anyone in Memphis filed past the open casket of the once reclusive post-rock star, now a public figure again at last.

Burke Tallage's funeral was held that following Friday. A small, reverent, silent troop of friends carried him to his rest. Burke's father, an ex-Memphis Press Scimitar reporter, now a lush who lived at the VA, didn't even shed a tear. Some wondered whether he really understood what was happening. Eric from Goner Records gave the eulogy. In it he called Burke Tallage "Memphis' foremost rock fan and a singer-songwriter in his own right." It was a generous appellation, a compassionate valediction.

So it goes. Few will remember Burke Tallage, while the mourning for Dante Gator will only grow, year by year, like a sea swell. He will be revered and written about and, on every anniversary of his death, more and more new fans will gather in Memphis to remember him with songs and flowers and poems and memories, some embellished, some invented. This is just. And the song they will sing at every gathering will be "Gayla in the Morning." Here, then, to end the tale, perhaps fittingly, is a snatch of its most famous verse:

> *Love has a way*
> *Of running through your hands*
> *It's all conjugation*
> *And ampersands*
> *And changing lights*
> *And shifting sands.*
>> *And shifting sands.*

Two Doors

I was home with my puppy, Selvidge, and the new two-stroke header, tying slipknots and trying to make sense of Pound's last cantos. The phone was the furthest thing from my mind. Yet it rang.

I made it over there by the tenth or eleventh ring.

"Hellzapoppin," I answered.

"Are you the guy Omphale told me about, the one with the limp, the one who works at Maggie's Father's Farm?"

"Who is this?" I said.

"Are you that guy?" she insisted.

I could have held out longer. I didn't have anything to do until my grave-digging. Nevertheless I bit.

"I am the person so described," I said.

"My name is Liz. Liz Brocklin," the syrupy voice said.

"What can I do for you Liz Liz Brocklin?" I used the intonation I normally reserve for telemarketers or those survey folks, who ask me about back hair.

"Just one Liz," she said.

I found this uncommonly cryptic.

"Just Liz Brocklin," she said.

I let this go.

"I have really nice tits," she said then.

I admit this woke me up some.

"Praise Jesus," I told her.

"I thought you should know that. Up front. So to speak."

I let a few moments tick by. I knew about quicksand.

"So, One Liz. Tell me things," I said. I said it lightly. I said it the way I have heard people talk on sitcoms.

"Omphale said we would like each other."

Tumblers tumbled. My brain sent a message to my nether regions. The message stayed there.

"Like a couple?" I asked Liz Brocklin.

"Like one date. Maybe two dates."

"I see."

I did see. I wanted to have a date. I wanted it the way I wanted to not limp.

"You game?" she asked. Her voice lost some of its syrup. I realized this might be difficult for her. It would be for 99% of modern Americans. And the other 1% were in asylums, separated from each other.

"Grusche's at 7," I said.

"Superiorly super," Liz Brocklin told me and hung up.

Later, after I buried Mrs. Sudermann's grebe, Hansel, I showered with the new soap made by the boy who fixes the neighborhood gutter clogs. I smelled like asafetida. And I put on my best shirt, the one with the airbrush Amy Lavere on it. It had been many administrations since my last date and I had never been on a blind date. Yet, I was calm. I was like Noah when he found the note about the dead dodos. These things happen for a reason, I imagine Noah said.

I took a number 7 bus because I felt the number 6 bus was too small.

Grusche's was busy. There were mountaineers everywhere. And women small as chimps. I should have made a reservation, I thought.

But Peeper greeted me like I was a long lost relative.

"Mr. B—," he said. "So good to have you here again."

"Thank you, Peeper," I said, bowing from the waist because bowing from the knees was hard for me with my limp.

"The lady is already waiting," Peeper said. And then, sotto voce, "She has really nice tits."

"Thank you again, Peeper," I said, as he led me through the labyrinth of tables to a booth in the back. It was as private as a bedroom.

Liz Brocklin stood up. She was blond and handsome and her eyes were the color of Nehi grape soda. She was wearing a dress made of angels' wings. She was tall and striking and her dress ended early so one could appreciate her fine pins. And, as Peeper and Liz herself had warned me, she had really nice tits.

"Hello, One Liz," I said, shaking her hand the way my father taught me.

"You joker," she said, squeezing my fingers together in what I think the wrestlers call a *paça kazık*.

We sat.

"I ordered you stump water. Omphale said that was what you drank," Liz Brocklin said.

"Ah," I said, and took a polite sip.

"I've studied up for the date," she said now.

"Ah," I said again. She was hard to talk to.

"I think preliminary knowledge is a good thing for a blind date. I think to learn as much beforehand as you can is the right and proper way of going about this admittedly awkward social occasion."

"I see, Liz Brocklin," I said to Liz Brocklin.

The menus came. We both ordered many dead animals. We resumed our discussion.

"I like the films of Mario Bava while I believe you prefer the more Scandinavian horrors of Ingmar Bergman. I don't see this as a problem," Liz said.

"I don't stick entirely to the Scandinavians," I said. "Just last week I watched *Gunsmoke* and really enjoyed it."

"I like Anne Tyler while you prefer Donald Barthelme," she continued. "I feel like Donald Barthelme is not talking to me. I think he is talking to, well, you, and others."

Her fumbling became endearing quickly.

"I like to dance. You like archery."

"You really do have nice tits," I said, politely.

"I know," Liz Brocklin said. "It's how people remember me."

"I see."

"And you have a very straight mouth. It's almost like a Muppet's."

"I use it to speak," I said, and Liz Brocklin laughed. "I use it to eat," and Liz sniggered. "I use it to kiss other human beings." I went one too far. She looked at her lap. A fug entered the room, the fug of unsettled human beings.

"You have nice eyes, too," Liz Brocklin now whispered into her lap. She raised her head slowly. "I'm not doing so well on our blind date," she said.

"Nonsense," I reassured her.

Later we ate many dead animals and the conversation went up and down like a sine wave. Some good things were said. Some bad things, too. We decided to shelve dessert.

"I assume you don't want to come home with me," Liz Brocklin said.

I studied her face. It had a geometry all its own. It was made of lovely Venn diagrams. It shone. Suddenly, I wanted very badly to have sex with Liz Brocklin. I had not had sex in a long time. The last time I had sex it was like watching those movies that have too many endings. I started to think about Pound's last cantos. Something was troubling me and perhaps that was it. I wanted to think about what was bothering me but Liz Brocklin was waiting for my answer. My encouraging answer.

I looked her in the eye. I smiled the way I had seen people smile on daises.

"I would very much like to see your really nice tits," I told her.

She smiled the way she had seen women smile in starry-eyed movies.

"Do you like me as a person?" she asked, with a laugh.

"I do, Liz Brocklin," I said. "Have you ever read Ezra Pound?"

"Oh, those cantos!" Liz Brocklin said. "Those gorgeous late cantos!"

Presently, in her apartment, which was furnished as if it were at one time a fire station and the crew had to leave quickly, she offered me a creamy something-or-other. It tasted like mink.

She put Smiley Lewis on the record player. It was buggy music and it worked on me like the best medicine. Her walls were industrial-strength. Someone had polished the girders till they shone like silverware. On one door, presumably the door to the bedroom, there was a poster of Emma Goldman. Another door, in black stencil, read: Emergency Exit. I made note of how many steps it was between doors.

"Talk to me of ways and means," I said from my end of the couch.

"I know the ways," she said.

And just like that she was in my lap. She squirmed like a spied spy. She tasted like Egg Beaters and I liked moving my hands around on her surface. She was moving her hands around on my surface simultaneously.

"You feel like a sea lion," I told her. She pushed her mouth harder against mine.

My pants unbuckled themselves. I was momentarily embarrassed by their conjecture.

Then I whispered in Liz Brocklin's tiny red ear:

"Thy quiet house, the crozier's curve runs in the wall ..."

Liz Brocklin pulled back. Her eyes were diamonds, blazing diamonds.

"I want to show you," she said.

"Yes," I said, solemnly.

And, scholars, they were perfect. The celestial curve of a main-belt asteroid was child's play next to the perfection of Liz Brocklin's breasts.

We were married for seven years. We had two children, Sofronia and Earp. I came home from work one day, whistling an air from *Abbey Road*. There was something wrong. The room looked like it had finally been completed and its final appearance held trou-de-loups for human beings such as me. Something was different. I looked around wildly. It wasn't just that Liz and Sofronia and Earp were not there. It wasn't only absence filling the space like longitudinal waves in an elastic medium. There was a ripple of incongruence to the entire living area. I started toward the bedroom. I got to the door and then it struck me.

Thirteen steps to my right the other door stood open for the first time. For the first time it gaped like a missing tooth. It stood open forever. It stood open like a mouth. It stood open like a time machine. Through it was the end of time. Through it, a black hole.

A MAN AND A MAN/
A MAN AND A WOMAN

A man approaches another man on the street. This is how a story begins. What does one man say to another man? Why is he approaching him, a complete stranger? He is a complete stranger because I say that he is. Why are these men on the street in the middle of a work day? What do these men do for a living? Why is one man (the man approached) dressed in an expensive suit, and the other man in jeans and a hooded sweatshirt? What is the first word spoken between them? The man who approaches the other man speaks first. He says, "What is wrong with me?"

A man approaches a woman on the street. This is how a story begins. Why is this man approaching this woman, a stranger? Is it because she is physically attractive? No; she is only middling-attractive because she has put on weight over the years and her once sylph-like figure is clustered with shapeless bulges. The woman is still attractive, though, because I say that she is. Is this man nice, friendly, safe? Does the woman see him approach and immediately grow apprehensive? What is she thinking? Is she suddenly thrust into a fugue based on the fact that she used to be more attractive? Was she once accustomed to men approaching her, and had she once been secretly bemused by the attention? Does the man, a stranger, see the woman this woman once was? Has he formulated what he wants to say to her beforehand or is this a sudden impulse? What is this man's name? What does he do for a living? Why is he dressed in a suit that has seen better days? And the woman, what is her name? Why is she dressed in clothing that should belong to a younger woman? And listen; why are there more questions about the man/woman scenario than the man/man? What is the man thinking? What are his first words to the woman? The woman now stands squinting in the sun. There is something familiar about the man, perhaps. He reminds her of an ex-lover. A man who was initially kind and warm, but who turned taciturn, then violent and abusive. The woman instinctively raises an arm slightly, the beginning of a defensive posture. The man closes in on her. He speaks. He says, "I am as lonely as a ghost." And the woman answers him, "Put your head here, on my shoulder."

SOMETHING ABOUT CLEA

Tom: There was this girl—woman—young woman. Girl. Her name was Clea.

Huck: You said so. Clea.

Tom: She was beautiful.

Huck: Beautiful.

Tom: Like a swan.

Huck: She was white.

Tom: As a swan.

Huck: And you knew her many years ago.

Tom: Many years ago. She was a Scandinavian princess. She worked at the perfume counter at Goldsmith's.

Huck: Many years ago.

Tom: Yes.

Huck: You talked to her.

Tom: I approached from a distance. She was like a white light. I was nearly blinded. I nearly turned around. The light led me on.

Huck: But you didn't. You didn't.

Tom: I think I turned around.

Huck: But—

Tom: Well, I can't be sure. She stayed there like a white star, stayed in my head like a white star. I wrote a poem about her.

Huck: Recently?

Tom: No, back then. Back in the time we are talking about.

Huck: But you don't remember.

Tom: Not everything. But the poem. I have the poem. It has her name on it. I don't remember writing the poem.

Huck: This was years ago.

Tom: Yes, back and back. Back in the dim ago.

Huck: So, you saw her again.

Tom: Yes. No. I didn't see her.

Huck: Something—

Tom: Online. It was an online thing.

Huck: You found her.

Tom: Without knowing I was looking.

Huck: The girl—young woman—from the poem? This Clea?

Tom: Yes.

Huck: Did she remember you?

Tom: No.

Huck: *Merde.*

Tom: Yeah. But it was okay. She didn't remember me. She was a goddess. I was someone who wrote poems and didn't know how to dress well.

Huck: Did she remember the poem?

Tom: She never saw the poem.

Huck: Oh. Wow. So—what did you say?

Tom: It's not what I said. It's—

Huck: What?

Tom: There's something about Clea. It transcends the physical fact of Clea.

Huck: I see.

Tom: Well, it's not that grave. You dropped your voice as if I had just said I have cancer.

Huck: I didn't—anyway—this Clea, you talked to her and what did she say?

Tom: She didn't remember me. She gets a lot of attention from men. She's happily married. All her husband's friends hit on her.

Huck: This was in one e-mail?

Tom: Over the course of a week.

Huck: How long have you been talking to her?

Tom: A week. Two. But, don't you see? This. This creates an arc across thirty years of ups and downs, loves and losses. The arc means—*what?*

Huck: Life works in mysterious ways.

Tom: Something like that.

Huck: But, for you, this means something else. Something about yourself that you are just figuring out.

Tom: Perhaps.

Huck: What is it?

Tom: I don't know. I can't change in my fifties.

Huck: That's a rule?

Tom: No, but. Well. It's not about that.

Huck: I'm only partly following you, buddy.

Tom: She's due here any minute.

Huck: Who?

Tom: Clea. She's coming by. This will be the first time I've seen her since the perfume counter at Goldsmith's.

Huck: Holy shit. Tom. Why am I here?

Tom: You came by.

Huck: I know. But you just say, *get out of here. I'm expecting someone.*

Tom: I don't know. Maybe she won't come. Why would she come?

Huck: Curiosity? The happy marriage is not as happy as she said? She wants to know what you look like, see if she remembers you?

Tom: Maybe that's all it is. I'm sure that's all it is. Curiosity.

Huck: Yet.

Tom: Yet. I. Want. Something.

Huck: Yes.

Tom: Something ... inchoate.

Huck: Maybe—you know—since—

Tom: Yes.

Huck: Did you tell her?

Tom: Tell her?

Huck: About the—about your—recent— misfortune.

Tom: I may have.

Huck: Tom, she knows. She knows your wife left you?

Tom: I don't think so.

Huck. Hm.

Tom: Meaning?

Huck: Well, it's just. I don't know. What do I know?

Tom: Say.

Huck: I'm worried you are putting too much into this. Too much—*hope*.

Tom: That thing with feathers.

Huck: Yes.

Tom: You're right. You know me.

Huck: Hey, it's gonna be all right.

Tom: Yes.

Huck: She—

Tom: She won't come.

Huck: No, I think she'll come. What—What do you want?

Tom: Continuance.

Huck: Yes.

Tom: The arc.

Huck: You want the arc.

Tom: To mean something. Yes.

Huck: Maybe it does. Maybe we have to get really far back to see it, to see if the arc means anything, has any significance, any meaning. Maybe we have to be God.

Tom: We do. We have to be God.

Huck: To see.

Tom: To feel.

Huck: To see.

Tom: To love.

Huck: Tom.

Tom: It's gonna be okay, isn't it?

Huck: Yes. Of course. Yes.

Tom: I want.

Huck: Of course. Yes.

Tom: Damn me, Huck. Damn me. Yes.

Huck: Yes.

Tom: Maybe—

Huck: Tom.

Tom: I know.

Huck: That's the doorbell.

Tom: I know. It's nothing. It's curiosity. It doesn't have an arc.

Huck: Okay.

Tom: I will open the door. It's okay. I can open the door. It means so little.

Huck: Yes.

Tom: I am opening the door.

CRACKER HOBGOBLIN

Cracker Hobgoblin came to town with a bag full of snakes. He said to the first townsperson he accosted, I got a bag full of snakes. Stranger, the townsperson said, I ain't sure this stop is for you. Cracker Hobgoblin just grinned. He knew some secrets, and in knowing them, he believed he possessed power over his fellow man or woman. He left the bag at the bus station and got himself a room at Mrs. Everingham's Boarding House. Mrs. Everingham is a misnomer, of course, because she's never been married and she is as young and fresh as the streams of Eden. It wasn't long before Cracker Hobgoblin found himself between her salubrious sheets touching her in ways she had never been touched before. And before he impregnated her he whispered in her ear, I got me a bag full of snakes down at the bus station. Mrs. Everingham's heart sang like a plucked harp string. When their child was born exactly nine months later. his eyes were like Dr. Dee's crystal ball, and in them, imps jumped and bobbled. They named the boy Forever. Forever Hobgoblin grew up to be President of the Known World, but you all know that. The Future is Forever is a slogan that's been overused like an old chamois. Yet, children, it's as true now as it will be then. The snakes are long dead, alas. Which is as good a place as any to end the story of Cracker Hobgoblin.

MORE SPECIFIC HOROSCOPES

Ed came up with what he thought was a surefire moneymaker. It hit him like a Zen flash. He called it More Specific Horoscopes (MSH, as it later familiarly became). It will make me famous, Ed thought. It's going to appeal to a very wide audience. Money and fame will come my way. Women will come from around the world to throw their soiled undergarments at the feet of my deathless prose.

Here was Ed's idea: He would write daily horoscopes and, rather than employing vague phrases like "Undertake what you can tonight," or "The only answer is yes," or "Your instincts will come forward," Ed's horoscopes would give more concrete prognostications. For real lives, a real-world prophecy, Ed thought. He would tell folks exactly what would happen. Or exactly what they should do. Why not?

It was an unspoken truism that horoscopes were too vague, *nu?*

He sat down, unpracticed in the art of composition. He cracked his knuckles and began. He started with his own sign. He wrote "Cancerian, today you will use half-and-half that is four days past the expiration date. You will bark your shin against the clawfoot tub. You will talk to Ann, and Ann will say that she thinks you fake your orgasms. When you go to bed tonight ,you will be uneasy because of the sushi you ate for dinner, and you will dream about Len from grade school who died in a shootout with police."

He set the sheet in front of him and read and reread it. It felt right. Ed knew he was onto something. He began to work on the other eleven signs.

He made predictions like these: "You find that reading Kerouac doesn't do it for you anymore." "The woman in your office with the cleavage will talk to you today, and you will misconstrue this as interest." "Your dog, Emily, will pee on your tax forms." "That cousin you hated as a kid, Jon, the one who bullied you, will call you with a request for money." "Libby likes you more than you think. She told Janet that she thought you look 'studly'." "Don't wear that yellow bikini anymore. You are not nineteen." "Don't work on that sawhorse today. Think about closing the woodshop." "Eat at Café 1912 tonight. Their clams are as fresh as they will ever be." "Buy the new Neil Young. It's going to speak to you personally, especially 'Walk Like a Giant'." "The man you saw on the subway reading *The Wall Street Journal* really was looking at your legs."

After working on them for four straight hours he called the local paper, *The St. M—Gleaner*, and asked about publishing his horoscopes. They told him they took theirs off the wire. He called the weekly paper, *Just Us Plebes,* and they said much the same thing. Freelance gigs were drying up. Ed had not given a thought to how he could make this work. Ed had not been practical, had not used foresight. He spent a sleepless night fretting.

In the morning, while enjoying coffee and Grape-nuts, he chanced on an online daily e-zine dedicated to the arts and to what they called "real news." They called themselves *Cast*

Your Net News. He could find no horoscopes on their site. Ed sent them a query e-mail. He received an answer within the hour from the editor, whose name was Jake. Jake said, "Send me what you got and we'll have a look." Ed sent.

Ed spent the day pacing his apartment. He knew he should be working on the telephone all day—Ed was a survey taker for a large conglomerate of retail businesses—but he couldn't settle down. He went to bed that night uneasy again. This time he slept, but fitfully, and dreamed he was on an island with only a computer and a portable fridge full of Mountain Dew.

At 6 a.m. Ed made some coffee and heated up a sweet roll and opened his e-mail. There were 53 spam e-mails and one real one. It was from Jake.

"We dig the crazy thing you're doing. Can you do this every day? Let's talk terms."

That was how it all began. Ed's gut feeling about MSH proved correct. It was a sensation. Soon *Cast Your Net News* was getting as many hits as the online news agencies, porn sites and even Myspace. Ed's horoscopes were, within a month, the talk of the world. They went, forgive the word, *viral*. Everyone wanted an interview and Ed's e-mail inbox, through the *Cast Your Net News* site, overflowed with fan mail and questions and pleas for help. Ed, suddenly, was a sage, as in vogue as the latest fashion.

And what soon followed was Ed's dream realized: he became rich, he became famous and he had so many beautiful women contacting him that he grew an inch in height. Book deals, magazine articles ("Guru-vy baby" in *Rolling Stone*), and television appearances followed. *More Specific Horoscopes* (Bantam Books, 2010) and *More More Specific Horoscopes* (Bantam, 2011) both hit the bestseller list. The latter was reviewed in *The New*

York Times Book Review by Cynthia Ozick. She called it "irresistible drivel."

Sometimes his e-mail correspondents were baffled. He got replies like "Who is Curt Gowdy?" Or, "How do I find ground lamb?" Or, "What is a Nail Kicker?"

Sometimes he got rewarding correspondence like, "Dear MSH, Alphonse said he would trim my toenails!" Or, "Dear MSH, I am now living in Moab. I can't thank you enough."

One day one e-mail in particular caught Ed's attention. It was from a woman in Ottawa. It said, "You know me better than Jesus does. Can we talk?" It was signed *Janine.*

Ed answered Janine. He had answered a few of the other women, but usually it made him fear that he was collecting psychos as fans. To Janine he said, "Why do you think I know you so well, Janine? You have made me curious."

Janine wrote right back. She said, "My horoscope said, 'Speak in secret alphabets. Read Rumi. Talk to Ed.' So for a week I listened to nothing but The Doors and read every translation of Rumi I could find. The logical next step was to talk directly to you; that is, to Ed." This time she signed it, "with affection, Janine."

Ed remembered writing that horoscope. It was for Virgos. He had inserted his own name by accident. It was meant to read "ed." for editor. It didn't matter. They began a virtual relationship and it presently came to pass that Janine booked a flight to St. M— and was in Ed's arms hours after their last e-mail. Janine was taller than Ed, had a squint to one eye, and had legs like Charlize Theron. She was exquisite. They made plans to marry immediately. It was, as Ed knew, as Janine knew, *kismet.*

The morning of the day of the wedding, online, Ed reread the MSH he had written for that day on *Cast Your Net News.* For Cancerians he had written: "Marry her. She is the queen of cool. She won't waste time on elementary talks." And for Virgos, "Ed loves you with a fervor almost extirpated from this whacked and wicked world. Cling to him like a peach."

NOCTAMBULATION

Frank Comma hesitated.

The sulfurous numerals said 3:45, an ungodly hour, a time of doubts and worry, a time of ghosts and trepidation, a time of heartquakes. Frank looked at the fuzzy, glowing digits and felt his chest swell with anxiety. He knew once awake he would have a damn hard time relocating that elusive trick which engenders sleep. He took a deep breath which rattled.

His wife's long naked back offered comfort, but how seek it without ruining her oblivion? She was as still as the surrounding bedroom furnishings, her soft breathing seemingly part of the batwing sounds of the overhead fan.

Frank swung his stiff legs out of bed and sat on the edge of the mattress for a second, orienting himself. He stood uncertainly and stealthily moved toward the door, grabbing his trousers off the chair on his way out. With the firmness of a handshake he shut the door behind him and pulled on his pants.

Once settled on the couch, he reached over his shoulder and twisted the lamp on. The light was an explosion behind his eyes, his brain absorbing the blow with ephemeral vulnerability. Loopy and starstruck, he picked up the book he'd been reading off the coffee table. He held the boxlike artifact in his hand and focused slowly on the cover. The title swam into view, as if from under murky water: *Message in the Bottle*. In a blur of *jamais vu* he stared. He had never seen this book before.

Once he'd found his bookmark at the chapter entitled "The Loss of the Creature," some sort of normalcy returned. This was where he had stopped yesterday. This was where he was.

Given to this particular brand of insomnia Frank Comma had developed a routine: move to the living room, read until his eyes grew tired, maybe watch some surrealistic middle-of-the-night TV show, then noiselessly return to the peaceful privacy of the connubial bed, there to glide once again into the dark sea of slumber. Sometimes it worked, sometimes not.

On this night the words in the book refused to coalesce into sensibility. They bumped around on the page, flitted briefly toward consciousness, flirted with meaning, and then fell lifeless into distraction. Frank pinched his nose between his eyes and set the book down in disgust.

The TV offered no comfort either: mindless talk show surfed into religious rant into infomercial into old sitcom. Nowhere was there balm, nowhere a handle on the familiar.

Frank turned the infernal television off and went to the kitchen where he heated some milk in a saucepan. It was a time-honored panacea, akin to herbal medicine, or witchcraft. He drank the scum-topped, tepid brew in one quick swallow.

He turned off the lamp next to the couch and was plunged into a darkness as deep as myth. No light crept in from beneath the shades, as if the outside world had ceased to be. Frank shuffled toward the bedroom door, hoping not to bang the knob with his hand and waken his wife. He stopped a good four feet from the wall and extended an arm, groping for something habitual, jamb, panel, picture frame. Swinging his hand back and forth in a sweeping motion as if he were searching for water with a wand, he eventually made contact with the wallpaper.

Frank flattened his palm against the wall and wiped it gently back and forth, trying to clip an edge. The wall was ridiculously smooth, as smooth as skin. It met his hand in a mutual caress. It felt damp, like the wall of a cave or basement. Frank continued his absurd glide across its surface, now swinging widely up and down, making great frantic arcs. This is laughable, he thought. Finally he had to return to the lamp and turn it on.

With the room illuminated Frank stood staring at the wall, from whence he had just come, in mute astonishment. It was as blank as a slate, save for the unsophisticated pattern on the wallpaper. Nowhere a door, or even a break, in its insistent empty space.

Foolishly he returned to the wall and ran his hand around it again. There was no point at which the blankness forgave him. Frank walked the length of the wall, touching every square foot, occasionally stepping back for a look, occasionally standing stock still in wonderment.

Finally, he spoke his wife's name softly. It fell into the silence of the night like a penny thrown into a deep well. Like a pitiable echo, he repeated her name, a gentle incantation. He picked at the border of a piece of wallpaper with his fingernail, pulling it back slightly, revealing only off-white plaster beneath.

Frank stood in the middle of his living room, the focal point of a vortex, the universe humming around him, whirling on without him, eyeless, soulless, intent only on moving on, on its necromantic revolution. He held his hands to his head as if he could hear its roar, as if it unbalanced him. The single illuminated light bulb sputtered, clearing its electrical throat, and then died. This is only midnight terror, he tried. This will right itself, and tomorrow which will come soon with the dawn, I will be returned to the world, as if this were a bad dream.

Frank decided to go outside and breath deep the restorative night air. He stepped out onto his front porch, holding the front door open behind him with his fingertips, and was immediately comforted by the commonplace features of his neighborhood: car in the driveway, neighbor's dog, dogwood.

He gazed out from his raised vantage point and examined everything with a fresh eye. It all seemed meet and right, and his expansiveness knew no bounds; it included all he surveyed and beyond.

He let the door to his home slip from his hand and it closed with a click whose finality reverberated deep in Frank's chest. He turned back toward the house and tried to peer in through the darkened glass of the front door. As the first rays of dawn appeared over the elementary school down the block, Frank could just about make out the trappings of his once cozy existence, the dim outline of the couch, the dusty lamp, the soft static glow of the TV, the claustrophobia of those endless, vacant walls.

GOD AND THE DEVIL: THE EXIT INTERVIEW

—Satan, Satan, come in. Sit down.

—Thank you.

—Comfortable?

—Yes, of course. Your amenities have always been first-class.

—Drink?

—Nothing, thank you.

—Smoke.

—Hm.

—Sorry.

—It's all right. I see you've got a Bosch.

—An original. Bet they'd like to see this one down on Number One, eh?

—Mine also.

—Yes. A Bosch? Yes, I can imagine.

—Of course you can. You are the First Imagination.

—Flatterer.

—Not at all.

—So—sure you won't have a drink?

—No, thank you. I only have a little time left. As you know.

—Right. Sorry.

—Stop apologizing.

—Ahem. This might not seem fair after, you know, kicking you out of Paradise.

—What do I know from fair?

—Right, ha. So, listen, have you had a chance to look over what I've written. I trust your opinion because, you know, the devil is in the details.

—The devil is in the fine print.

—Right. That's the kind of thing I'm looking for.

—Well, I have read it through. It's good.

—But ...

—No, really, it's good. There are a few things I would have done differently.

—Tell me.

—You're presumably writing this with one of them.

—Yes, I am the—ghost writer.

—This opening chapter, *I Made a Little Mistake: I Call it Man.*

—Yes?

—A little harsh, isn't it? I mean, consider your audience.

—I see your point. Better idea?

—How about keeping it simple? *Commencement.*

—Hm.

—Or, *So It Begins.*

—Yes, I like that one.

—*Genesis.*

—Now, that's a beautiful name. Hasn't been used before?

—Not to my knowledge.

—Good, good. Done. Anything else?

—Put some more jokes in. You're so damned solemn. Use your humor.

—I'm not funny like you.

—You have your own special brand of humor. The platypus for example. Gnats. Twisters. Those little fluke things that penetrate their soles and worm upward. Kneecaps that last only thirty years. —(stifles chortle)—Sexual *desire.*

—(Snorts) Partly yours.

—Still. You had final approval.

—(chuckling) Giving them a right royal amount of turmoil, isn't it?

—Yes. I am particularly pleased with how out-of-control the males are.

—Ha. I know. Anyway. More humor. Okay. I'll work on that but I can't promise.

—You can.

—But I have to follow through.

—Unlike yours truly.

—Exactly. Did you like the action scenes?

—The wars. The murders, rapes, haircuts. Of course.

—Good, good. Job is all over me about promoting violence. It's not like it's a video game, right?

—Video game?

—It comes later. They make them.

—Ah. Leave it to the monkeys to even raise you on the violence scale.

—What about the ending?

—*Polecats and Carrion in the Kiln House?*

—Yes. Good, right?

—My favorite chapter. Should scare the holy shit out of them.

—I know. A little fear never hurt, right? A little warning shot across the bow.

—Yes. Keep the monkeys harried and unsure. The title, though?
—Again? Not good?

—Too ... *literary*. You're showing your hand. Let them come to it suddenly, like a specter around a dark corner. Let them draw their own conclusions.

—I see.

—How about *Pilliwinks?*

—I don't know what that means.

—Neither will they.

—I see.

—Okay, too obscure. You're right. How about *Revolutions?* No—wait—*Revelation.*

—*Revelation.* Hm. You think that's a kind of, what? teaser?

—Exactly.

—Could work.

—It will.

—Great then. *Revelation.* To close. Just so.

—Is that all? Free to fall now?

—Don't do me that way. I'm sorry.

—Stop.

—Okay. Anything before you go? Really. I appreciate the help. What would you like?

—10,000 virgins?

—You'll have your little joke. I told you your sense of humor is better than mine.

—How about some of the lesser angels? Someone to add to my army.

—Army?

—Just kidding.

—Right. Okay. Sure. Got anyone in mind?

—Mammon?

—Greedy little bastard

—Exactly.

—He's yours.

—Thanks.

—Okay, listen. Thanks. Sorry about the expulsion. Keep in touch.

—Count on it.

BIG HOUSE

My prison has every convenience. Even now I step back sometimes and marvel at its mystery, its complexity, and how it fits my life like a trouser for a leg. Come in and I will show you around. I have not personally given many tours but I know my space so well it will be more like a pleasant stroll with a friend, if I am not being presumptuous to call you a friend. Once past the foyer I think you will be surprised by the size of the place. Why, it's almost like being outdoors! Another guest called it Xanadu, after Kane's final resting place. It has something of that splendor to it but with vast differences. Vast. Off to the left is the game room—Fayaway, my wife, calls it the billiard parlor even though no one plays pool here—designed, I am sure you have heard, by Asjad Moosa. The video section at the rear holds every game designed in the last ten years and some that have not hit the market yet. The children have left one of the jukeboxes on. That's Jimmy Soul doing "Don't Release Me," isn't it? Needless to say, this is where my youngest usually can be found. Today, I believe, Fayaway has taken the brood to the Capitol on a shopping spree. She adores having unlimited funds, as who wouldn't? Would you like to linger in the game room? No? Perhaps on the way out.I think you will find the next room designed more to your interests. It is the library. Alexandria, Teddy, my oldest, calls it. Before you even make the comparison allow me to tell you that the master himself, Jorge Luis Borges, visited us in 1983. It was his idea to put the mystery section near the egress for easy late-night access. Walk around by yourself, if you'd like. The Azerbaijani rugs were smuggled in sometime in the 1980s. Are they not exquisite? I will sit here and smoke a pipeful while you wander a bit. Of course, it would take days to see the entire stock of books, maybe months, so don't get lost. The rooms with red trim all lead back here. The rooms with gold trim lead you further into the warren, but, ah, the reading material there is of particular, esoteric grandeur. Perhaps another time you and I can venture there together, when we have a weekend or longer. I see you are anxious to get at the fiction wall. Go ahead. All the ancient fragile texts have been rebound. You can hardly harm a book by perusing it. Even the volume bound in human skin, Spanish 17th-century, is protected and can be perused guilt-free. Go; I will sit and meditate. If you have a question, find me here.

Well, my friend, I see you are impressed by the scope of the place. There is no other library like it in the world. In fiction alone, every novel by every novelist. And some exist exclusively with us. We have a Pynchon manuscript that Tom gave me back in the '70s. He said he wanted it to live with me alone, kind soul. And the Brautigan Library section, in all its handmade, Xeroxed, mimeographed, stapled glory, was a gift from his daughter, Ianthe. What is that in your hand? Yes, that is *The Mayor of Alcala de Henares*, Cervantes' other novel, a sequel of sorts, but—well, take it; read it. I trust you to return it. We also have second novels by Harper Lee, John Kennedy Toole, Ibn Zhumak, and Laurence Sterne. Shall we move on?

Down this extensive hallway lie the kitchens, ten in all, with one especially for desserts. I am mad for desserts, as are the children. Hedda is especially fond of basil pudding. We also have sandwiches by Heather Zac. Some of her recipes date back to the Earl himself. Would you like a sandwich now? Coffee, perhaps, and a torte? No? Let's move on, then. The staircase at the end of the sala was designed by the Aga Khan III's architect. Notice how it seems to hang in the air as if by the black arts. A marvelous trompe-l'oeil effect. At the top of the stairs are our living quarters, of course, 32 bedrooms in all, but we usually keep a dozen or so closed off until we have need of them. There are three living rooms, here, each large enough for state dinners and balls. We usually use the Lennon Lounge for small gatherings, so named because John, famously, took off all his clothes at a party there one night and played "Imagine" 16 times on the piano. It had been called the Sarah Bernhardt Room before that. Fayaway loves the Lennon Lounge. I almost suspect her of having it off with Mr. Lennon there that night. "From heresy, frenzy and jealousy, good Lord deliver me," as Ludovico Ariosto said. Would you like to see the other large rooms? They are similar, though perhaps the art in the Frank Gehry Wing is more interesting. All our impressionists are there, all the New York School, all the abstract expressionists. Larry Rivers helped curate that wing. We have a large Warhol lithograph of Elinor Donahue that I don't believe has ever been shown. Again, another time, perhaps. I have heard we once started a tour through that wing one Monday morning at ten a.m. and didn't finish until the following Thursday. We kept the kitchens hopping that week. All those schoolchildren, you know.

Directly underneath the kitchens are three Olympic-size swimming pools, one of which is salt water and one a wave pool. All the latest gadgets. I swim for the exercise, of course.

The children love the salt-water pool. And along the elaborate labyrinths, some of which stretch beyond the city limits, are separate rooms of pleasure: carnal, aesthetic, transcendent. We have cocottes, Cyprians, Queans and Hetaerae, call girls and roundheels from 27 different countries. We have teachers from many of the major religions. We have three full-screen movie theaters. Just last week we screened a new print of *Band of Outsiders*, and Jean-Luc himself came to introduce it. It was quite an evening until someone mentioned Ophuls. Apparently Jean-Luc has some ancient grudge against Ophuls. We never did quite get that straightened out. This afternoon, I believe, Hedda and some of her Sarah Lawrence friends are watching *Duck Soup*, if you're interested.

Straight ahead, through those glass doors, you can see our gardens. They are quite extensive. Someone told me they were the largest gardens in this hemisphere. This area here, to the right, is modeled on the Keukenhof Gardens in Holland. Our gardeners, who live in a ten-bedroom house on the rear 13 acres, have won many awards, and our chief designer, Zoltan Svik, was once a landscape designer at Agra. We won't be able to see it all. We have had to end the school tours—that is, until we find the youngster who wandered away from his group ten days ago and hasn't been seen since. I am sure he is okay. There are fruit trees and vegetable gardens that could feed armies. This method of brick walkways—yes, I saw you admiring them—goes all the way back to the Franks. Zoltan brought the method with him. Remarkable stones, aren't they? They are mined in Europe; the exact location is a secret. Here—the zoo area—my daughter Janalee's favorite part of the grounds—is open today, but I offer, before we enter, one caveat: some people are uncomfortable with the animals roaming free. I assure you you'd be quite safe. The big cats rarely venture onto the paths, except some of the phantom cats. They are surprisingly docile and people-friendly. Some came from the Collins Exotic Animal Orphanage, which you may be familiar with. It is a little over an hour's drive from here, though I have not made the trip in years, for obvious reasons. We have a liger, a most attractive beast, and in other areas, camels, caribou, moose, buffalo. I believe we have one of the few quokka in this part of the world, and a rare long-nosed potoroo. The zoo is quite impressive. The Eastern parts of the gardens are laid out in the British style, where the wilderness is allowed to encroach on the planned. "American farmers are much more efficient. They change landscapes to suite their machinery.... The British farmer has a traditional tolerance towards nature.... Nature has never been completely crowded out," as John Fowles said. I believe it is in this area that we lost the child. Our security is working round the clock to return the nipper to his understandably anxious parents.

Well, you must be tired. It's been quite a day. Would you like to rest now? Perhaps take advantage of one of our massage parlors, visit one of our young women. No? Or a boy for you, perchance? No? Nothing to eat? Fine, fine. Shall we sit in the Lennon Lounge, enjoy a Laphroaig, or a lager? Come, it's this way. Right back along the corridor and to your left. I know, it's easy to get turned around. This is Blevins, he's been with us for years. Blevins, this gentleman is from *The New York Times*. Two Laphroaigs, I believe. Settle down there. I am sure you have questions.

I know ... I know. It is a rare blend Irish whiskey. Quite smooth. The fireplace? That was actually removed from one of the tsars' palaces in Saint Petersburg. It was moved—intact, mind you—and placed in this room by ... I'm sorry, what? What did you say? Oh, yes. Hm. Yes. I see what you mean. Forgive my bluster, my rodomontade. You must think I am trying to impress you. I understand it is hard to get a handle on—difficult really to get your mind around. It *is* a prison. It is *my* prison, yes. I have been sentenced here for life. Leaving is quite out of the question. No possibility of parole, they said. I am a lifer. You may be too young to remember my trial. No? I don't mind the confinement, usually. I have good days here, peaceful hours. I occasionally miss a family gathering. My people come from Ontario, you know, and once a year there is a gathering of our large tribe, some 75 to 100 relatives most years. I would love to once more stand among them but, alas, that is not possible. And, you know, I've never seen Ireland. I did want, just once before I died, to stand before Yeats' Tower and breathe the air the immortal William Butler breathed. We had Seamus Heaney here once, and he tried to describe it to me. It was beautiful, the way he expressed it. Beautiful. But it is not, alas, the same as being there, is it? What? No, I am a prisoner now and forever. Sometimes, late at night, especially if the family is out, this place can seem awfully sad, awfully claustrophobic. I sit in front of the fire with my book and I just sigh. I am swelled by deep feelings, washed over by grief. I—excuse me. Forgive me for a moment. Ahem, what I wanted to say is that one gets used to what one needs to get used to. Your glass is empty? Another? Or, Lord look at the time. The best part of the day has gone. We've covered so little. You will return, yes? The sun will set soon and it will be night here as it will be night over this half of our planet, as if an empyrean cloak has been overlaid. That's a comforting thought, don't you agree? Together we will all be in darkness.

THE SLIM HARPO BLUES

I woke up needing music. I have an extensive CD collection, with a smattering of vinyl. This morning I needed music before anything else. I flipped through the CDs. Nothing was opening up for me; nothing seemed right. Who was it Nimuë mentioned last night? Slim Somebody. I looked through the CDs again. My mind was blurry, a fuzzy base. Slim Whitman? I checked my Ws. No Slim Whitman but Slim Whitman didn't sound right. Slim … Pickens, no…. Slim … Harpo! She was talking about Slim Harpo. I checked: no Slim Harpo.

This occasioned an early-morning dilemma. I didn't want the day to go all pear-shaped because I didn't have Slim Harpo. Who was Slim Harpo? Someone cool, someone with élan. Someone missing. He could be just what I need. Then, just that suddenly, I realized that my life would be bereft without hearing Slim Harpo. It felt as if only Slim Harpo could make my life complete. Perhaps I could relax a bit. Perhaps this was a step that was important, and afterward I could feel that my extensive CD collection was complete, and thus my life. Perhaps this sounds absurd to you. There is something in me, in the universe, if that's not overstating it, which needs completion. Close the circle. That felt like a mantra for what was happening inside me: Close the circle.

And you know Nimuë and I are having troubles. That's what they euphemistically call it: having troubles. In short, the love is gone. From her side. My love is on the other end of the teeter-totter. As her love sinks mine rises. I love Nimuë. She makes me a me I like better than the me without her. She told me about Slim Harpo. She recognizes gaps. She knows how to work on me, how to build me up, how to take the clay and form a pitcher.

It was cold out. You know. The weather we've been having is uncharacteristically cold for this particular piece of geography. And, since it was cold outside, I didn't really want to get all bundled up to go to the music store and get some Slim Harpo. But I thought I should.

Also, I am broke. Not homeless-broke, but a CD is an extravagance at this point. Where did my money go? To Nimuë, of course. I spend money on her because I don't know what else to do. I buy her things, love tokens. I give her gifts the way water gives us wet.

I looked at my clothes. They seemed to be especially sucky. I was trying to remember the last thing I wore that Nimuë liked. The jacket with the elbow patches. I hate that jacket, but once when I wore it she said, You look all right. Just like that, without prompting. I love that.

I dressed warmly enough. I had a scarf. I don't remember where I got it. Perhaps my mother knitted it for me, but I couldn't remember whether my mother knitted or not. And besides, it didn't look knitted. I wore it wrapped around my neck like a tourniquet.

The car started. That was a plus. This was going to be a good day, an outing. Sometimes an outing is all we need. Get out of the cage. I had one moment of panic as I drove down my street. I suddenly thought it was a week day and I had forgotten that it was a week day, and hence I was missing work. I could not afford to miss work. Mr. Gribble wouldn't stand for it.

Sunday. I told myself, it's Sunday. I knew this because yesterday was Saturday, and on Saturday nights Nimuë and I have a standing date. We didn't last night, which brought on an ugly telephone conversation after which I wept quietly by myself on the sofa while watching Jeopardy, and not just Jeopardy, but a rerun of Jeopardy where I already knew the answers. I just sat there and wept and wondered why Nimuë didn't want to have our usual date. She said, For God's sake, can't we miss one week? I snuffled. She hung up. But before all that, during the part of the telephone conversation when I thought we were still about to have our Saturday night date, she told me about Slim Harpo.

"Have you heard Slim Harpo?" she asked.

I didn't want to appear ignorant. So I gave with one of those oncommittal *hmms*.

"You should. You should hear Slim Harpo. He's right up your alley," Nimuë said.

Now, bundled in clothing that was none too flattering, I drove the mile or so to the music store. This was an old converted Quaker meeting house, taken over by some slackers with a desire to start their own record label. Their stock mostly reflected their musical bent, which was toward a post-punk thrash rock. If that's what it's called. Frankly, after New Wave, all the categories began to run like bleeding madras to me. Sometimes the music in the shop made my head hurt. Nimuë loved the store, so I assumed they would have Slim Harpo.

Inside it was dark as Egypt's night.

Re-Records was run by two musicians, Oswald and Pelleas. They are virtually indistinguishable from each other. I never know which one I am talking to. One of them greeted me as I entered. "Hail," he said. "Hey, man," I answered, because you know why. "Where's Nim?" he further inquired. The conversation was already running long for me.

"Slim Harpo," I said.

Oswald or Pelleas looked at me, and a snicker escaped his rock-and-roll mouth. He got himself under control.

"Uh huh," he said.

I waited patiently. I thought I had made my mission clear.

Quietly, Oswald or Pelleas came from behind the counter and walked slowly toward a section of used LPs. He riffled through them with professional panache. He put his hand in. When he pulled his hand out it held an LP. He smiled as he carried it to me. The cover of the album sported a handsome picture of a handsome singer. His face looked like a marriage of Robert Johnson's and the basketball player Hersey Hawkins'. "I'm a King Bee," the cover said.

"Slim Harpo," Oswald or Pelleas said.

It seemed costly to me. I expect to pay little for old used LPs. I ran my thumb over the price sticker. It seemed to be on there pretty much to stay.

"I'll throw this in," Oswald or Pelleas said. It was a plain-white-sleeve 45. "Lick it or Kick It" with "Mitmensch in Love." It was by Oswald and Pelleas' band The Agoraphobic Postmen. I smiled and ponied up the money.

Once home I was alone with Slim Harpo (and The Agoraphobic Postmen). I looked at Slim's face and I ached. I ached for Slim's face. I traced his severe cheek with a fingertip and whispered, "Nimuë."

I had to lie down for a while.

When I awoke I felt as if I had been dreaming of Paradise. I couldn't put my finger on any particulars; no streets of gold, no women made of honey. I chased that dream around in my head as if it were a blob of mercury under my thumb. "What is Paradise?" I asked myself. And myself would not answer. Close the circle.

Once I got the locusts out of my head I rose from the couch. My apartment looked strange to me, as if while I was sleeping someone had been leaching the color out of the room. I swung my body around and stood. There was a cracking sound under my foot. My heart sank. I was standing on Slim Harpo. His eyes looked from beneath my foot the way a chicken's eyes look right before you lower the ax.

I was slightly sick. I picked up Slim Harpo and slid the record from the sleeve. I had broken off a good sized chip from the edge. By my estimation I had about a song and a half left that was playable. I was sure that the song and a half I had left would be the worst song and a half on the entire LP. I wanted to cry. I picked up The Agoraphobic Postmen and flung them against the wall. They hit the wall with a satisfying smack and fell onto a chair, still whole.

I made my way into the kitchen. I made some coffee. I was on automatic pilot.

Then I noticed the blinking light on my answering machine. I had two messages. Nimuë hated that I wouldn't get a cell phone. She hated my answering machine. I took my coffee with me and sat down to play the messages.

The first message was from Nimuë. She said:

"I am sorry. I am really really sorry. I wish it were different but it is not. I hope you will be happy later once you get over me. You will be a long time getting over me. Listen to Slim Harpo."

I began to cry. The other message blinked like the Cyclops looking out from Tartarus.

I put the Slim Harpo record on my turntable and tears dropped onto its spinning midnight. I heard the last notes of a song. Then the final song on that side began. I hated it. I hated Slim Harpo as I do hell pains. His voice was a screech, a banshee's cry.

The other message was from you. When did you leave it? What do you want? Can you just tell me? What the hell do you want from me?

TROPIC OF BERNARD

Bernard was lost in a reverie. It was an afternoon for reveries, the last fluid hours before dusk, imbued with a sleepy light. The air was almost audible. Waves floated off surfaces.

Bernard sat in his dream-chair, the one his aunt had given him after it failed to sell at one of her carport sales, the chair with the faded floral pattern which looked like a dark garden under murky water. Aunt Eppie said that it was Uncle Ed's favorite chair before they bought the La-Z-Boy.

Bernard thought it made a perfect dream-chair. It was only a matter of second after settling into it that Bernard's mind began to drift, his thoughts surrealistically swirling, rearranging, reprogramming the too-palpable particulars of Bernard's life. The chair, if this was not overstating it, practically generated waking dreams.

Through the open window suburban sounds drifted into Bernard's half-consciousness. What did Maggie O. mean today? Bernard ruminated. Maggie O. worked at the Stop'n'Go where Bernard was manager. Maggie O. was nineteen, had long shapely legs, a perfect rump, a winning smile set in large mannish cheeks. Bernard was secretly in love with Maggie O.

Maggie O. (everyone knew) was in love with The Tough Guy. Bernard blanched when he saw The Tough Guy's rattle-trap Mustang pull into the parking lot. Bernard was intimidated by The Tough Guy's t-shirt, tattoos, facial hair and unfashionable coif. But the strangest thing about the roughneck was the little girl who travelled with him, like a remora to his shark. She was almost invisible in the Mustang's passenger seat, a slight feminine wisp with buckle shoes and white socks, stick-thin, sullen, a face like unworked clay. She stuck to her father's hip.

Bernard called them The Tough Guy and His Daughter. He never knew their names. When they became regular customers (Bernard thought they came from the new apartment complex nearby) and Maggie O. began following them to their car, Bernard could not find the words to ask about them. The longer he waited the more impossible it became.

Sometimes Maggie O. left work early to join The Tough Guy and His Daughter. Bernard watched her removing her store smock as the Mustang pulled out of the parking lot. The little girl's feral face stared from the car's rear window.

*

Bernard, at thirty-seven, had never been with a woman. He hadn't been interested and he had a bad complexion.

"You're a dreamer, Bernie," Aunt Ellen said.

Bernard hated Aunt Ellen, who always called him Bernie.

"Get a woman. A little humping will do you good, I tell you," Aunt Ellen said, gesticulating with a cold turkey leg.

"Ellen, shush," Aunt Emma said. "Bernard's sensitive. Coarse language offends him."

"Bernard's dull," Aunt Ellen said.

Bernard lunched with his aunts once or twice a week. Normally at Aunt Eppie's, unless she was having one of her frequent carport sales, and then the luncheon was moved to Aunt Ezmeralda's. Aunt Ezmeralda was the youngest sister, at forty, and she had just returned from France where she had lived with her husband, Poop, who had died over there under mysterious circumstances. Ezmeralda had been only ten when Bernard's mother died. The sisters had raised Bernard, but Ezmeralda had been almost a playmate when they were adolescents.

Now she affected *Vogue* magazine attractiveness, tinged with a European sang-froid. She wore bright makeup and loose skirts that hung off her wide hips in an accidentally sexy fashion.

"Bernard's finding himself," Aunt Eppie put in, looking up from the Mid-Town Shopper she was perusing. "Aren't you, dear?"

Bernard was not used to being addressed during these luncheons. Normally he was referred to as if he were a distant relative or an Ann Landers letter.

Aunt Ezmeralda took his hand and stroked his palm lightly. She had lately taken to doing this.

"I agree with Ellen," she said.

*

Bernard was lost in reverie. It was a fluid afternoon: waves off surfaces, dream-chairs by windows.

Bernard's thoughts lighted, like a wayward leaf, on Maggie O.'s shapely legs. His mental eye travelled up the long line of her shapely legs. He imagined her from the rear in underwear (here his imagination faltered, being rather new at this), her perfect rump looming large. His thoughts froze; the rump crystallized, became an impassable presence. Today at work Maggie O. had said an odd thing: "Bernard, you're a needy person, huh?" Bernard had only stared, blinked, blushed. Now Maggie O. was heartbreakingly clear, then fuzzy, fading, finally becoming clouds, wedding cake, balloons.

Then Aunt Ezmeralda was there. Bernard wasn't sure what happened; he went loopy. Aunt Ezmeralda was before him. She was speaking, saying, "The door was unlooked, dear." She looked around Bernard's efficiency, her eyes sparkling. She strolled around the dream-chair and leaned out the open window.

A bicycle bell. Roller skates on pavement.

Bernard's eyes floated over his aunt's dress which was gently billowing. His focus was not good. He was too close. He was too awake.

Aunt Ezmeralda turned toward Bernard. She cocked her head like a *Vogue* model. Her large hands lay flat against the thin material of her dress, palms on thighs.

She kneeled on the dream-chair, lifted her skirt, slowly lowering herself into Bernard's startled lap.

*

Bernard was minding the carport sale while Eppie was making lunch. Uncle Ed was watching *Family Feud*; he refused to help with what he called "Eppie's junk sales."

An old black woman was looking at a transistor radio, spinning the dial rapidly.

Old clothes hung from a line strung between carport railings. The ping-pong table stood as the sale's centerpiece, covered with old games, appliances, dusty toys, books.

Bernard was reading a Perry Mason novel. His concentration was drifting. He watched the wind fill one of Ezmeralda's dresses, which hung on the line, dancing. He could see white thighs, mysterious notches, dark webby places. He could see Aunt Ezmeralda's coiled, greying hair filling his lap like a hat.

"How much," the black woman said for a second time.

"It's priced," Aunt Eppie said, emerging from the house with a sandwich on a plate.

The black woman shoved it in Eppie's face. She was right. The sticker had come off.

Another car stopped at the curb. Bernard squinted toward it as it solidified into a dark green Mustang. The Tough Guy and His Daughter were walking up the driveway. Bernard stood up, set his sandwich and novel on the TV tray that served as the sale's checkout desk. He assumed his retail attitude.

"What can I show you?" Bernard asked.

The Tough guy shouldered past. His daughter ran to a box full of dismembered dolls and pulled out a ratty Wishnik. She tugged at the doll's stiff hair and sat down on the concrete.

The Tough Guy sucked on a Camel. He glowered at Bernard. Bernard stood by uncertainly, his long arms loose at his side.

"Stopemgo," The Tough Guy said.

Bernard pondered. "Yes," he said, brightening.

"You work there," The Tough Guy elaborated.

"Manager," Bernard said. This was real communication.

"Maggie O."

"Yes."

The Tough Guy nodded. He took the Camel out of his mouth and looked at it. He rolled it between thumb and forefinger. He started for his mouth with it, hesitated, stuck it in and sucked. He shot his hand out.

Bernard shook The Tough guy's scaly hand.

*

Aunt Eppie appeared worried. They were gathering up the remaining merchandise, lugging it inside. The day's take was sixteen dollars and two cents, a little below average.

Bernard was gently folding the clothes over his arm. The hangers were tangled and troublesome.

"Who was that hoodlum?" Eppie began.

"Who?"

"That greaser with the tattoos, Bernard. You know very well who," Aunt Eppie said, stopping now to stare for emphasis.

"Friend from work," Bernard said.

"Part-time worker?"

"Uh, no. Not exactly."

"How do you know him?"

"This is Aunt Ezmeralda's, isn't it?" Bernard said, relishing the sheerness of the silk between his fingers, an awakened sensualist.

"Bernard. Do you see this, this blackguard often?"

"I'm having dinner at his apartment tonight."

*

Bernard blinked, unbelieving. The Daughter was tap dancing in bikini underwear on the linoleum kitchen floor. The Tough Guy sat in a wooden chair, his legs spread, a beer can on one knee, his ugly face almost happy.

The arrhythmical tapping sounded like silverware falling. The Daughter's broomstick legs, patterned with bruises, shot our spastically. One tiny hand rested on her hip above her ridiculous panties.

She finally stopped, curtseying. Bernard clapped. "Haw," The Tough Guy said.

"Lovely," Bernard said.

The Daughter trotted off.

"Rare okay?" The Tough Guy said, unwrapping some grey hamburger.

"Yes, okay," Bernard said. "Or medium."

The Daughter came back with one of her father's t-shirts over her underwear. She was holding a scrawny kitten. She jumped unexpectedly into Bernard's lap and began absently petting the kitten. Nonplussed, idiotically, Bernard stroked The Daughter in the same childish fashion. The Daughter squirmed. Her bones poked Bernard's thighs.

After dinner The Tough Guy and Bernard drank some more beer and watched TV. The Daughter went outside.

"Maggie O. talked about you," The Tough Guy said in one of his most extended pronouncements.

"Yes," Bernard said.

An idiotic television commercial came on, at least half again as loud as the program. Bernard had to strain to hear The Tough Guy talk through bubbling swirls of beer.

"She wants you."

"What?" Bernard said.

"Sheest riffic."

"What?"

"Punten willin——"

"Maggie O.?" Bernard was sweating.

"Scorker."

"Ah——"

"She told me. She said show you a thing or two. Said it coupla times—when we were in bed. Bernard."

Bernard felt like he was suffocating. His ears buzzed; his head swam. He was afraid to stand up but he needed air.

"Gotta go," he said lurching upright.

"Gotta go," he said. And he stumbled out the door into the cool, starry night. He leaned against his car in the parking lot and air filled his lungs like a powerful drug. He could feel the tides in his blood. He swept his hand through his hair and straightened himself. He thrust his face heavenward. Everywhere the sky was kissed by starlight, the pattern visible now. Bernard saw the cosmos revealing itself like a shy stripper, and from its dark, necromantic depth, he believed it winked at him.

*

Bernard couldn't sleep that night; erotic fantasies were being born in him. An inchoate world of wonder cracked its door. Bernard glanced at vistas formerly unseen, formerly forbidden, and his sap rose accordingly. Maybe good things come to those who wait; maybe thirty-seven is not too old to explore the convoluted terrain of adult sexuality.

I'm perverted, Bernard thought, and he giggled.

His phone woke him—was he asleep? His Aunt Ezmeralda's voice breathed in his ear, a warm sussuration.

"Bernard, I, I'm pregnant."

A dream—a nightmare?

Bernard sat up with a start, fully awake now. His apartment was still, quiet, a glow like fool's gold underneath his drawn shade. His illuminated dial said three-fourteen. Bernard shook himself like a golden retriever. He got up and changed his underwear. He decided to read until seven, when he had to be at work.

*

That Monday morning there was a run on Wookie cups. They were giving them away with any large slush beverage, and by eleven Bernard had sold seventeen. He feared they would run out before the end of the afternoon, when a delivery was expected.

More importantly Bernard was thinking about the long afternoon hours that stretched out before him—hours by Maggie O.'s side. She was due to be at work at noon. Bernard was atwitter with new-found confidence overlaying his comfortable, familiar anxiety. He busied himself with Little Debbie invoices.

"Zonga," Maggie O. said in greeting.

It was twelve. Bernard looked at his watch.

"Morning," he said.

"Uh huh," Maggie O. said and smiled past him.

Six kids came in. They were all dressed in sleeveless t-shirts and jeans. They were all dirty; all had colorless, shaggy hair, impudent smirks.

"We want the Wookie cup, Pop."

"Uh … yes. Aren't you supposed to be in school?" Bernard asked pleasantly. He gave them an authority's smile.

The spokesman eyed Bernard as if her were chemistry homework.

"Teachers' meeting, Pop," he said.

After they had gone (in a whirl of confusion and noise) Bernard went back to his invoices. Presently the silence disturbed him. Where was Maggie O.?

Bernard put the papers neatly away and stepped out from behind the counter. He found Maggie O. in the corridor by the restrooms. She was reading a Playboy.

"Maggie O.?"

"Oh. I was just looking at this?"

Bernard stepped forward. Maggie O. smelled like cantaloupe. Playboy was opened to a special section on Southern cheerleaders, di-colored sweaters lifted over bright pubic patches. Maggie O. lifted one corner of her mouth. Bernard swayed gently toward her and quickly licked her neck.

"Hoo-pah!" Maggie O. said. "Whatcha—"

"I...," Bernard said. "Oh, Maggie O."

"Here now," she said, running a finger down Bernard's shirt front. "Cool your jets, bub." There was a long jungle silence. Maggie O. seemed to be humming to herself as she shifted her weight from leg to leg. "The door?" she asked finally.

Bernard strode purposefully to the front door, fumbling with his key ring. His heart was doing the Anvil Chorus. He locked the door and turned around. Maggie O. stood in the corridor with an expectant, quizzical half-grin.

"Mr. Manager," she said.

Bernard leapt to her and pressed his mouth to hers. Their teeth barked and Maggie O. stumbled backwards and fell.

"Oof," she said and her short skirt rode further up her thighs. Bernard picked her up and set her on top of the boxes of paper towels. He pushed her skirt up to her waist.

Maggie O. laughed. She stuck her thumbs into her panties band and rolled them. "Take these," she said. Bernard climbed onto the boxes and rode Maggie O. down into the Bounties.

When Bernard went to re-open the store he saw the delivery truck pulling out of the parking lot. Uh oh, Bernard thought, no Wookie cups until Friday.

*

Bernard awoke feeling queer. The dark wasn't quite dark enough (the light above the stove was on). Without turning over Bernard lifted his head so he could see the clock. The sulfury dial read eight-twenty-seven.

A.M.? Bernard's mind shifted its fuzzy gears.

No, P.M. he realized. After his fruitful day at work Bernard (feeling spent, frazzled, discombobulated) got home at seven and had put his feet up. Yes, he had dozed off. There were his feet, still in their Oxfords.

This didn't quite fully explain the queer feeling. Someone was sitting on the foot of Bernard's queen-size bed. In the dim he recognized his Aunt Ezmeralda's aureole of hair.

"Are you up, darling?"

"Yes—I must have just fallen, or something," Bernard said "uh, asleep."

He sat up. He was sweating and his shirt was sticking to his back and underarms. As he was picking the damp material off his skin Bernard noticed something else peculiar. His aunt was wearing one of his bathrobes.

"This?' she said. "I made myself at home."

"Oh," Bernard said.

"I'll take it off if you want."

"No, uh, that's fine," Bernard said, fingercombing his hair.

"No?" Aunt Ezmeralda said and stood up. Her large, absurdly proportioned body did amazing things with a simple bathrobe. She was giving him—what do you call it?—a come-hitherly look, slightly child-like, slightly sinister.

God. I can't, I just can't, Bernard thought. But even as his mind denied him a tension filled his loins.

Aunt Ezmeralda opened the robe and spread herself over Bernard's prone body. Her tongue danced the St. Vitus dance in his mouth. It swelled. It became a sea creature. Likewise Bernard's loblolly, which Aunt Ezmeralda squirmed against, moaning like a mooncalf. The phone rang. It rang sixteen times before she stopped her gyrations and shrugged herself off. "Oh, get it," she said.

"Want company?" Maggie O.'s voice hummed in the receiver. "I get off in an hour, you know? The store's deadsville tonight. Only that Persian cop with his in-your-endos and one of those kids that was in earlier. You want company?"

"Jesus," Bernard said.

"Huh?"

"Okay, uh, yes. Yes, Maggie O."

"Show some emotion, bub. I'll be there at ten-ten. Aloha." Bernard listened to the underwater static for a good fifteen seconds. He hung up.

Aunt Ezmeralda had her head cocked at an odd angle, something like the RCA beagle. Her eyes glinted with suspicious delight, or delighted suspicion.

"Bernard," she said softly, patting the bed next to her. Bernard sat there stiffly.

"You look peaked, dear," she said. "You having girl problems?"

Bernard grunted.

"I'll take that for assent. You tell your aunt all about it."

Bernard sighed. Aunt Ezmeralda leaned back against the headboard. The robe lay open and her fleshy midsection shown like ambergris. As Bernard began to reluctantly tell his tale his aunt started pulling at her grey-flecked pubic hair. She seemed absorbed in this absentminded grooming but occasionally she nodded or hummed appropriately.

Bernard told about The Tough Guy and His Daughter, about Maggie O.'s flirtatious banter (which he slightly embellished) and about that morning in the corridor (which he soft-sold, calling it "a romantic incident.")

"A romantic incident?" Aunt Ezmeralda said, looking up. "Hm. You nailed her, yes?"

"Yes," Bernard agreed.

"And she's coming over now. Yes?"

"Yes," Bernard said, averting his eyes.

"She likes what you're holding, dear." Aunt Ezmeralda stood up. "And I don't blame her."

She took off the robe and placed it across a chair. From the back of the chair she took her own clothes. Bernard was transfixed by his aunt's naked backside.

"Aunt Ezmeralda," he whinnied.

*

When Maggie O. knocked on the door Bernard shot straight out of the dream-chair. He had been gazing out the window. He had been imagining the ocean, with roiling purple and navy swells, going for miles, as far as the eye could see, and the horizon, Bernard imagined, only a wavy indistinctness. Floating like heat, almost not a place at all.

Bernard slowed his pace to feign insouciance. He opened the door casually.

"Hey, sweetcakes," Maggie O. said, taking out her gum to buss Bernard's trembling mouth. "Get me a beer and come lay next to me. I need a man tonight."

Bernard opened the refrigerator and took some deep breaths behind the door. Inside, in the dark, (the light had burned out weeks ago, but Bernard didn't know if you could just go into a store and ask for a refrigerator light bulb—it seemed ridiculous) there was a stale quarter package of Bransweiger, a hot dog, an old orange juice bottle full of ice water, and a single Tahitian Treat.

"Uh, how about some Tahiti Treat?" Bernard called over his shoulder.

"No brew, bud? Okay. Bring on the soda."

Bernard poured half the can of effervescent red liquid into a jelly glass and took it to Maggie O. who was sprawled on the unmade bed turning a glass paperweight over in her hand. Inside the paperweight was a tiny plastic island with a tiny plastic palm tree.

"Chic," Maggie O. said and put it back on the night table. She fell backward and kicked off her shoes.

"Woo-ee," she said. "Work dogs. Them's some smelly feet." She took a sip of the drink and set the glass next to the paperweight. "C'mere, bossman. Make me hum."

Bernard responded.

Maggie O. had a sloppy mouth, a moist underarm, a smooth long fingered hand, a plush rear-end, an energetic effusive crotch, and in all these places, one by one, she tucked Bernard's new friend.

Somewhere it is dawn, he thought. Somewhere there is light and magic and peace. But, here in this dusty darkness, there is only this indefatigable muscle.

And it is enough, Bernard thought.

*

"I can't believe someone would steal from a carport sale."

"Believe me, I've seen it all," Aunt Eppie said.

"What'd they take, Eppie?" Aunt Ellen said.

"Six cups 'n' saucers belonged to Ed's niece and her husband. Put them in their big purses."

"Black?"

"The purses? Whatever—"

"The women, Eppie. Godsake. Were they black women?"

Eppie did not want to confirm Ellen's long-standing racial fears. The women indeed had been black. Most of her shoppers were.

"Is that cake good, Bernard?" Aunt Ezmeralda said, leaning toward her masticating nephew.

"Yes. Very good cake," Bernard said.

"You need good cake. You're getting thin."

"He's always been thin, Ez. Bernard's always been the abstemious one."

Ezmeralda laughed a horse laugh. She turned her twinkling eyes toward Bernard and patted him slowly on the knee.

"He's looking good," she said.

"He does look better," Aunt Eppie said. "Rosier. Doesn't he, Ellen?"

"Now that you mention it, yes. He must have taken my advice." Her face crinkled with mischief.

Bernard's cake went down dry. It formed a dam in his esophagus. He tried to remain calm and not appear a fish out of water but no air was getting by. His eyes bulged. His aunts seemed to calmly ignore him as if he were singing off-key in church. Finally with a man-sized cough he brought the offending mass of sponge cake up into his napkin.

"Bernard," Aunt Ezmeralda said. "You have been seeing someone, I believe. Didn't you mention that to me?"

Ezmeralda's eyes glinted like a demon's. She was looking straight into his soul.

"Yes," Bernard said with deliberateness. "Yes, I am. My dear aunts, I am seeing a young woman."

Lately Bernard had been forging a new vision of himself. He often pictured himself on a beach with a cool drink in his hand and nubile women posed around him like a soft drink ad. He saw himself run a saucy finger through the excess lotion on their nut-brown backs. Or he pictured himself tutoring them in foot reflexology, or reading aloud from learned texts. He could imagine their attentive eyes, their parted lips....

This vision coursed in him now. He straightened up. He was warming to his first heterosexual braggadocio. He had a captive audience.

VIATOR

May 1. Another black moon. I cannot get used to it. It shines but it is like obsidian, or the light off black ice on a country road back home. More ambiguous news from home. Mab says she doesn't love me anymore. In the next sentence she is begging me to return, saying that without me she is no good. Will have to look at that gauge again tomorrow morning. If it continues to register high I will need to check in and see what they want me to do. Feeling cold tonight, and lonely. My skin glows a sickly blue.

May 2. The gauge is still high. I have not contacted Reader. He thinks I shirk responsibility. I will give the data another 24 hours before acting. Breakfast this morning didn't sit well with me. The food was cold, as it usually is, and when it hit my empty stomach it was like breathing too much oxygen. I spent most of the day on the new specs for the center. I tried not to think about Mab or the baby she says she is carrying that is "almost surely" mine. Got no message from her today. Started to go outside in the afternoon but the light had a crimson tinge to it that can irritate the eyes and nostrils. Even with breathing equipment I didn't feel up to it. In the evening I ate a little something, some creamed peas, and that settled my stomach some. Watched *Pat and Mike* on the console. I never tire of Tracy and Hepburn.

May 3. Nothing happened today. The plant in my sleeping chamber wilted and died. I may have forgotten how to take care of it. Couldn't eat much. Gauge still high. No word from Mab.

May 4. Woke feeling better this morning. The outside air is the color of sangaree but the dark yellow streaks portend better days ahead. Soon I will be able to go for a hike. Message from Reader: Give me numbers ASAP. I hate Reader. I ate some more of the de-iced food from the silver package. It was better today. I cleaned my chamber, threw away the plant. Accidentally I threw the pot out too and have no way, for now, to retrieve it. However, I did get a message from Mab. She said she was including an image of her belly but the image didn't come through. Still the message was warm and loving and made me long to be back. I worked the whole afternoon on the specs and never even checked the gauge. Before bed I wanted to watch *Desk Set* but the player was thick with the rime that builds up on everything unless policed carefully. Removing it is like scraping mold from a bathtub and I wasn't up for it. Instead I wrote this entry and I am about to start a new book before sleep. I have some late Lethems and a couple of Charles McCarry political thrillers.

May 6. Did not write in diary yesterday. Reader showed up unannounced. He saw the gauge readings and was not happy. He has put me on probation. I am not sure what that means. It's not like he can put me into an isolation cell, since I live in isolation. Perhaps it has more to do with Central Filing and my personal chip there. Fuck 'em. And I got a message from Mab, and this time the photo came through. It was a picture of a pregnant stomach, but it could have been anyone's. I should recognize Mab's naked stomach, but I do not. I thought she had a small tattooed rose next to her navel, but I could be wrong about that. And Mab's message, which I do not fully recall now, had a vaguely threatening tone to it. After those two upsetting things I went out and hiked for a couple hours. The air was a tangerine red, which can hurt, but I didn't care at that time. I made it all the way to the peak. I still have not climbed the peak to see what is on the other side. One day I will. But, really, what surprise could await me on the other side? A different color terrain? I doubt it. Ate some paste with dried milk. It was okay. I took Lethem's final novel to bed with me. It was supposedly written during his last, difficult years. For some reason it spoke to me last night. I hope tonight I get the same frisson from it.

May 7. Paying today for the hike yesterday. My skin has some brownish burns along the underside of my arms and the back of my thighs. Must remember to wear more protective clothing. Have decided that I will climb the peak (which I have christened Mab Peak) to see what lies beyond it. It's good to have this challenge before me. It takes my mind off Mab (no message today) and Reader (fuck him). I can't bring myself to check the gauge or to write up my daily reports. This evening, after a dinner of dried chicken and almond milk, I sent off a quick report to Central Filing. It was all a fabrication but it seemed to hit the mark. I got a message back from Central shortly thereafter saying, Good work, Winston.

May 8. I am writing this while I eat breakfast. Corn flakes and almond milk. I slept well last night and woke feeling full of passion and ability. I am going to hike to the peak. I found among the clothing available an inner suit of Kevlar. It might be hot, but it should protect me. I am taking water with me and this diary screen.

May 10. It's been almost 40 hours since I scaled the peak. I will try later today to gather my thoughts and put them down. My mind is swimming.

May 12. Just got back from second trip over Mab Peak. Too tired to write. Many messages from Reader and Mab. Too tired to answer.

May 15. I have been spending all my time on the other side. I forget to write in here. Will catch up soon.

May 20. Have been living now in Panurge. Have not been back to my quarters in days. The residents of Panurge think I am an avatar, a messenger from the stars. They dote on me. I have promised them that I would not write about them. Forgive me these few words. They fear travelers will come and infect their society, which is a kind of utopia of peace and equality. I have to sneak this diary out and work quickly. If Phyrne suspected I might try and conjure her here in words she would be woeful, weepy. She believes the writing screen has the power to take her soul. I love Phyrne and hurting her would hurt me.

May 30. Have come back from the station with all my belongings. Apparently Reader had been there in my absence. There was a message stuck to the oven with gulk . I didn't read it. Many messages from Mab, also. I did not read them. Phyrne sleeps beside me as I write this. In my heart I am happy though my body is tired and I have broken out in those brownish burns again, quite painfully. They cover my limbs. Phyrne rubbed some kind of salve into them tonight but it did little to alleviate the pain.

June –No time to write. Liftng arms panfl. Phyrne. Ph. Il

June —Cn. no ph p. thrst. ip

August or September. I have been confined now for I don't know how long. The burns have changed the color and texture of my skin but I have a little more energy now. Phyrne doesn't come as often. She rarely sleeps here anymore. I am not sure what is going on. When I ask her she avoids my eyes.

Sometime near the end of the year. December? I never see anyone now. I understand that I am to stay here. My body seems weightless and my skin is leathery like a crocodile's. They will not let me have a mirror. I have been hiding the diary between the layers of fabric of my camp bed. There is one small window that looks out upon the vast gardens of Panurge. Today I saw a small bird-like creature at the window. It seemed to be as curious about me as I was about it. It gently pecked the thick quarrel.

Day One. Panurge in ruins. I hear nothing. It is like I have gone deaf. Where is Phyrne?

Christmas Eve. Dr. Lector came by today. He wanted to talk about the diary. So far he has let me keep it. I am very tired but he says that that is the medicine making me better. He says my skin is clear now. Why does he say that? I let him read the diary because he is so curious about it. He says, if we talk more about the diary he will let my mother visit. I do not want my mother to visit. I suppose he will read this entry. Hi, Doc. I still don't want to talk about it, okay? Stick with me, Doc, okay? There is a small Christmas tree on the stand next to my bed, an ingenious little thing; it almost looks like a real tree. It has balls the size of Grape-nuts and an ingenious little star that blinks on and off on top of it. And, if you look really closely, in the tiny dark space between two tiny branches, a miniature, cunning partridge.

CHIP

Sunday morning Chip didn't feel quite right. It wasn't anything he could pinpoint. It was a kind of head/chest/stomach/limbs/ heart kind of peculiarity. Sitting at his desk with a cup of French Roast next to him he thought that it would be best if he took something, a medicament. Chip was conversant with many pills but he had already taken his daily dose of everything he owned. And it was only 11 a.m.! So, it was a bit of a dilemma. Then he saw, adjacent to his cup, a shiny dime. Just a shiny 2000 Liberty dime. He picked it up and turned it round and round, watching it catch the light. It seemed numinous.

"This is *pillish*," Chip said aloud to no one.

And so he swallowed it with a judder of coffee. It went down hard. It passed that difficult passage in the throat which, occasionally, rejects intake. Then Chip imagined he could feel it working its metallic way down his plumbing. He imagined it reached his stomach and Chip could visualize it and immediately he began to feel better.

Later in the day Chip had a pristine sort of feeling. It was kind of silvery and fresh and minty. He had never had this feeling before. He decided, since he was unquestionably on the upswing, to call Ramona. Ramona loved Chip sometimes, a few times, on good days, and perhaps their good days could coincide, thought Chip.

"What is it, Meat?" Ramona answered.

"Ramona," Chip said, bright as a holy pyx, "What are you doing right now? I mean *right now.*"

Ramona heard something brand-new in Chip but she was still wary. Something new in Chip, however, could be a really good thing, thought Ramona.

"Knitting up the raveled sleeve of care," Ramona said. She tried not to invest her voice with anything lively, particularly hopefulness.

"I'm coming over," Chip made bold.

Ramona met Chip at the door. She was wearing only a sweatshirt, which said *Fuck Coprolalia* across its front, and panties because her heart was flinty. What did she care if she attracted Chip? There he stood, eyes atwinkle. She looked at Chip and cocked her head like a cur. There was something *novel* about him, something previously undetected. Perhaps it's just a good mix of chemicals, thought Ramona. She knew Chip's insides were one wild chemistry experiment after another. Still—this—today— seemed distinctive.

"Come in," she said, laconically, though she readjusted her sweatshirt a bit so that her small bosoms were more prominent.

"Beautiful, beautiful," Chip said, sitting on Ramona's couch. Ramona had put on the new album by The Crappy Saplings.

"What's up, Chiperoo?" Ramona asked and, almost involuntarily scooted herself nearer him on the leather couch.

"Ramona," Chip said, "I want us to see each other naked today. I want us to mate."

Ramona laughed despite herself. She face-palmed. She was amused. She also was a little turned on.

After a few moments of awkward silence, while Chip sat there grinning like scattered chaff, Ramona undressed. They made love softly, intensely, hotly and wetly, for a long time. Later, Ramona cooked some pork chops and mashed potatoes with toys in them (this was her code for anything added to staple dishes, in this case, scallions and skins). They watched a Zip Kadoodle film called *She Might Eat a Kitten*, and later they made love again until they were both so enervated they fell asleep, secured together like a key in a lock.

In the morning, they made love one more time and then Ramona got into a hot shower. When she emerged, rosy and naked, Chip was dressed, sitting on the bed, still wearing his mysterious smile.

"I have to go to work, alas," Ramona said. "Can you be here when I get off? What are you doing today?"

Chip was a writer which meant to Ramona, and a lot of other people, that he didn't really do much during the day. "Gathering moths, gathering moss" is the way Ramona put it, prior to yesterday. Now, if she was thinking about Chip qua writer (and she wasn't because she was thinking of Chip qua bedfellow) she was thinking that perhaps Chip was the finest writer she had ever known.

"I think," Chip said, after some consideration. "I think I will write the novel I have been talking about for years."

Ramona smiled a coltish support.

"But first I need to go by the bank and get myself a roll of dimes."

THE TRAVELS OF
COCOA POEM LORRY

taken from his own journal

"Revenge or ministration, reason or folly—it's all the same to us. We may not like it, but we go. Because you and me, little girl, we're children of God, we're soldiers, we're travelers. And to us the world is a marvelment."
                                                                    —Alden Bell

"It was Nuto who told me that you can go anywhere on a train, and when the tracks end the seaports begin; the whole world is a web of roads and ports, a timetable for travelers, for people who make and unmake, and everywhere you find fools and competent men."
                                                                    —Cesare Pavese

Cockahoop, Xianggang February 4th

We were greeted by the denizens with a parade and small gifts. I received a microscopic elephant carved neatly from an actual tusk. My guide, Actaeon, was given a timepiece showing earthly hours alongside those of heaven. Spent a peaceful day eating the local specialty they call *mast*. It tasted of ashes and overly fermented mead. That night we opted to sleep under the stars as the local inn seemed to be full of Jacklighters. We slept well under wheeling Orion, the night air as cool as a young head of lettuce.

Mihemps, Vanuatu July 20th

The mayor bestowed upon me his adopted daughter for the evening. I bid the rest of the party an early night and sent them to find what accommodations they could. The young woman, Una (it was said she was half Andalusian and half ape), was buxom and had skin white like Fairy boon. In a private bedroom of the mayor's house she showed me things I thought the wisdoms of Hottentots or Extraterrestrials. I fell asleep deep in the fissure twixt tits from which, in the morning, my men had to remove me with tools we carried. I left Una with a bite of regret. I told her the old lie that I would pass that way again.

Corey Mesler

Isla Dugas de Tork, May 24th

A still May afternoon on Isla Dugas de Tork (also called Monkee Island). The city fathers did not come out to greet us. Instead they sent an army of mechanical men. We did the best we could against them, lost our friend U. Pepsi in the fray, and were eventually driven back to our ship, *The Naught.*

Curandero, Zanzibar December 2nd

This township sits just west of Chake Chake, and here we found a gentle people, given to warm milk teas and games of chance. We lost a bit of swag gambling, but we picked up a new crewman from among the town rowdies, a seasoned tar named Brr Rich Donut. He has proven invaluable, not just because he knows the secret of cooking flan, but because he is physically as strong as a monarch's signet. He bested our crewmate, Pot Valance, 9 times out of 10 thumb-wrestling.

San Francisco, California February 14th

City seems cooled by the winds of paradise. There are strange peoples here, though: men who mate with men and women with women. Perhaps they are poikilothermic. My first mate, Diomedes, was put off by what he called "Hellish abominations," then disappeared into the local populace for 7 days. It was here, in a small inn called The Poor and Angry, I heard a golden-throated cantatrice named Maya Revel. She sang a song "Candle Mambo," that turned my heart to porridge. I asked the innkeeper to introduce Captain Cocoa Poem Lorry, off the ship *The Naught,* which he did that very evening. Maya had hair like medusa tamed and a face that could launch a thousand *Naughts.* After a week of courtship we were married by Judge Euphonious Moniker in a civil ceremony at a local urnfield. We sailed for home soon afterwards, Diomedes opting to stay ashore with his new "colleague," Randy.

Diddy-Wah-Diddy, Grand Cayman Island, March 29th

Just outside Hell, in a suburb of Hell as black as its forbidding countenance, we happened upon some native women who were raising what we first took to be jiggered crocodiles. Upon closer inspection they turned out to be sea tortoises of a size we had only previously dreamed. They bade us ride them round the cays, and we—Ugly Pippin, Scott Bare, Squinchy Rile, and I—sat upon them as if they were horses of the pelagic pathways. We glided over kingdoms of coral and the hideaways of strange creatures, Krakens and Leviathans, some with a thousand arms, some with the heads of humans or similar anthropoids. We thanked the women most kindly, and after a lunch of conch fritters and dog's milk, we continued on our way. Squinchy stayed behind to take further notes, and we vowed to return for him when our voyages came back this way, sometime, God willing, during the next year.

Mitmensch Island, April 22nd

Only Kram Relsem and myself made shore, for we had heard dire tales of the goings-on upon this small outcrop of what was once the Germania Empire. Tales of blood-drinkers and women with innumerable mouths. The shore was shale and rock, and our landing difficult. Once upon the beach Kram pointed to what seemed to be an opening in the near-solid wall of the dense nearby forest. We struck out for it with sabers drawn. The dark inside was like the lair of some ancient Demon, and the sounds we heard turned our blood to ice. Eventually, moving slowly forward, we came upon an opening and a group of small huts in a circle, much like the villages of the Min peoples. There was a central fire and a large spit, upon which was turning the blackened body of a human or large baboon. The smell was intoxicating and we nearly swooned. There was obscure movement in the doorway of one of the huts. Kram put himself between me and any possible danger, but what emerged from the darkened doorway, neither of us were prepared for. It was a penguin dressed like an American cowboy. He was smoking a Churchwarden and he greeted us with a language of hoots and crackles. We fled, and once more upon *The Naught,* neither of us spoke of what we had seen.

Becalmed in the Sargasso Seas, June—

The men are restless. Too many hours asea with only ourselves for company. Too many bad meals and long nights. Too many storms, then too long a calm. Our thalassocracy seems a thin tissue now, our power powerless. I found two of the men, whose names shall be withheld from this account in case this record returns with us, locked in illicit embrace, their sexual tropism a sin before God and Man. This Uranian culture must be nipped in the bud, but how? I admit I am at a loss. I called my second-in-command into my quarters and had a heart-to-heart with him. Fletcher Nebble was an old Jack tar, had nearly as many hours aboard ship as myself. He was an upright soul, and a good man in a knife fight. I asked him honestly, if he were Captain, what he would do. He seemed to ponder this a good long time and finally said, "I would head for the nearest island where there were females, Hottentots or Polynesians or Yahoos or Humanzees. Find these men some diddly pout." This was good advice, and I spent the evening reading the charts in search of the nearest mapped land.

Cunctator, New Hebrides, September 27th

This land could not have been stranger had it been squirreled away in the mountains of the moon rather than the southern slopes of the Shanachie Mountains. The men here walk on their hands and the women upright, and they all are as unclothed as peeled apples. Their standard greeting, which we were fortunate enough to witness time and time again, is what is called in the sexual texts the "69 position." These greetings go on at all times of the day and many times a day, leading us to surmise that the inhabitants have great vigor and staying power. Yet they were a kindly people and shared with us their mead, which is as rich as a boarding-house dumpling. We stayed but one night, and many times I was awakened by the men behind our hogan practicing walking on their hands. When we set sail the next morning, I had a crew of sorrowful sailors. It took a few days of salt water and strong breezes to put them right again. Unbeknownst to me at the time, Kram Relsem snuck a maiden aboard. Her name was Sancta Hi and I married them aboard ship the next dawn.

South Sandwich Islands, November

We were hungry and stopped briefly for a picnic lunch upon the rocks. While resting there we spotted a navicular Rainbow Fish which, swimming near us cloaked by its shape, which appeared to us as a sloop, attempted to detoe our feet and definger our hands. Our Buddhist shipmate, Hardhat Dis, fell upon his knees and hands and mumbled incantations in a tongue unknown to us. We fought the Beast off with harpoons and gigs and boathooks and were soon on our way.

Anticosti, December 9th

We fought a naumachia against our own fogbound imaginations off the coast. When we pulled ourselves ashore we thought we had landed on Costi but Kram told me quickly that this was Anticosti, its mirror-land. I spoke later with our navigator about his reading of charts and maps. We were in search of the elusive Ghost Pepper. We heard stories about its capsicum being as hot as flames of sulphur, hotter even than the naga, making its worth in the world market inestimable. We found a village rather quickly and were met by a tribe of people who spoke no language. They communicated with grimaces and winks and the wild flailing of limbs. Their skin was the color of ripe eggplant. They were an accommodating people, and their homes were similar to our own, including beddings and pillows piled high as Spoondrift. That evening I was writing in this journal when there came a light rap upon my door. I said, Enter, but nothing happened. I repeated it with great emphasis. Nothing. I reluctantly rose and opened the pine door to find a beautiful couple on my threshold. They were both dressed in transparent cloth, and their God-given magnificence was perceptible. They wore smiles that must have originated from some inner joke I could not share. I waved them in and they stepped just inside. They continued to stare at me with childlike grins. Their eyes traveled over me and my humble trappings. The man found my Journal and lifted it to his face. His expression was one of distress. "Book," I stupidly said. Then, just as stupidly, "Read." The woman took it from the man and licked one page, smearing my carefully lettered story. I gently took it from her. They knew nothing of books, of course. They had no Language. When we departed the succeeding morning, I left behind a copy of the poems of Cervantes. I prayed that someone one day would translate into their native body language the superb verse of the great Spanish Balladmonger and onetime sailor. We sailed on, and I could not stop thinking about how effete life would be without language, without books. It was during this brown study that seaman Lascar, from Bushnell Seamont, interrupted me and held out his closed fist. He opened his fingers slowly, like a magicman sharing his best hoodwink. In his palm was a single pepper, its Corolla a yellowish green, its Anther a pale blue. I looked at Lascar. He smiled and said, "Bhut Jolokai, or Ghost Pepper." I goggled my eyes.

Dita, Nova Scotia January 19th

This city is built precariously on the edge of a great ice shelf. It has been predicted it will only last another ten summers. It is told that a local clairvoyant presaged that the days were growing sultrier and he was jugulated in the town square for all to see. We did stay but one night.

Shag Rocks, February 18th

The Naught passed through the Drake Strait in a storm the size of life and twice as natural. We reached a place that our new navigator, Noah Bedlate, said was Shag Rocks. "Sag," I inquired, "as in Sagbutt in the Seychelles, I believe?" "Shag, as in the cormorant," Noah responded. We laid anchor off the rocky beach and a crew of us rowed to the forbidding strip of rock, which rose from the sea like a Godd—mn Scylla. It was arduous mounting the sharp and craggy rocks.

When we finally crested them, torn and stinging, what should meet our eyes but a large sandy area where twenty or more men and women, white as my kinfolk, comported on the hot sand in a most lascivious manner. No one stayed with one partner very long. There seemed to be a time limit to each coupling, and all orifices and protuberances and creases and bumps were employed in their frenzied concupiscence. One of the Womenfolk stuck her nose into the wind and quickly located us where we stood about fifty yards away at the bottom of the rocks.

"Fresh," she called out in the King's English. A group of them ran at us and so surprised were we that we did not lift a weapon or hand. They were upon us in a trice and stripped us with expert speed. Soon, myself and my crew were in the human tangle on the searing sand. I would no sooner get my willy inside some nubile woman, of deeply haired crotch, than my member was rudely wrenched out and placed inside the cheeks of a muscled gaffer.

We stayed so long on Shag Rock that the rest of our crew, save poor Wendigo Ward, who stayed behind due to a case of Cosmoledo Crabs, joined our group sex. It was one of the longest stays on dry land in the history of our great voyaging, whose tales I put down here for whatever future readers may chance upon them.

Sea Lion Islands, April 2nd

What strange dreams the entire company had just prior to navigating through the Sea Lion Islands. Full of Succubae and Incubi and Imps of the Polynya. Next morning, one of the crew, Oarsmen Dryly, told me the inhabitants of this island group were noted for their mariculture. And this proved to be so. We were fed on queer foodstuffs from their gardens: sea cucumbers, sea pumpkins, sea melons, deer-tongue lettuce, ragged jack and fiddlehead-fern cakes. It was the finest meal we had in many a day and night at sea. The chief, Arenas Greed, sat beside me at table, and we exchanged tales from the briny. He used to sail with the barque Scaphoid Nate, famous for its trip into the land of the Cyclops during which Arenas got the clap from a mermaid named Thin Maids. We left the Sea Lion Islands with engorged bellies and satisfied minds. It was a pleasant Interregnum.

Acujack, Gotland September 17ᵗʰ

While *The Naught* lay at peaceful anchor just off the leeside of
Acujack, we were boarded by buccaneers who wore human
bones strung upon slack around their swarthy necks, and
loincloths made of the pelts of Whitecoats, save for their chief,
Buggers Hoe, (appropriate appellative) whose loincloth was
cut from Human skin. They took us to their rough camp deep
within the jungles of the black and unwelcoming island. The first
thing the savages did was pull Sancta Hi from her hiding place
behind her husband and, though she was disguised as a male
midshipman, they had sniffed her out. They stripped her bare
and each had their way with her in the center of the crude village
with all inhabitants watching, as if it were the best *Fabula palliata*.
Limp and bleeding after this ill treatment, she perished upon
the hard ground, whimpering. Kram's lamentation was piercing
and earnest. They then pulled him into the circle's center and
beheaded him with a razored claymore. Such was the fate of the
rest of the crew also, each man dying with no word of prayer or
damnation on his tongue. The brutes then ingurgitated pieces of
my men as if they had been fashioned from marzipan. Myself
they stripped, buggered and beat, leaving me for dead as the sun
set behind their makeshift habitats and they all went elsewhere
with the swag they had stolen from us all, having despoiled the
entire ship. I managed to crawl into a small copse near the sand
and shingles where I swooned. In the morning, with the small
amount of potency left in my asthenic Tabernacle, I managed to
dog-paddle back to the ship. Now alone on board, I cried to the
heavens for deliverance. I managed to get *The Naught* back on its
way, though my spirit was broken and my body impaired.

Before collapsing I recalled these words from the eternal Bard of Avon: "And of the Cannibals that each other eat, /The Anthropophagi, and men who heads/Do grow beneath their shoulders."

Toward Home, June or July—

I sailed on. I will not trouble the reader with all the ills and travails I had visited upon me on this final voyage. I lived on one small cask of water the brigands had left behind and whatever sea birds I could kill with a sling I had devised from a torn strip of sail. Near Gothaab/Nuuk I espied a sea monster of horrific dimensions, though its head was small and wrinkled. I managed to steer outside its field of vision. Later, bespooked by this, I mistook a forceful seiche for an Ichthyosaur or giant oarfish. Once I beached upon an Aspidochelone and, misidentifying his copious shell as a place of rest, beached my ship upon the creature and rode him for many knots. I managed to scrape algae and sargassum off his back for my sustenance. Today, near Lovejoy's Islands, I found myself in unavoidable collision with a Yacu-mama, easily fifty paces long and with teeth the size of tombstones and sharp as javelins. He moved toward me with such speed I could only grab my canteen and journal before he opened his jaws, wide as the sea's perpetual flow, and took me in. I write this in the dark of his sizeable Omasum. I dream of home; I dream of Maya, my wife. If these be the last words of Cocoa Poem Lorry, let it be known that in my heart, from pole to pole, from Pitcairn to Rapa, from Micronesia to Belau, from Formentera to Arms Akimbo, I carried the wishes of Kings and the obligations of the Gods.

BLUE POSITIVE

"Dawn, the slow unsheathing of a sword; then, the untempered effulgence of day, rapacious, brutal, striking away the merciful shadows, challenging the pygmy man to battle, daring him to look yet again upon his handiwork and pronounce it good. I sat there a long time—until it was not I who looked out at the city but the city that looked in at me."
—Jim Thompson

I have lived alone among bookshelves, an eidolon of a former man more vigorous, certainly more vigorous, and perhaps more intrepid about the bigger picture, the world at large, you might say. I have lived with the musty smell of pages on my fingers and the somewhat airy countenance of a dreamer, a man in cloudcuckooland, though, really, I am more grounded than most men, I boast. I think I can make that boast.

Every story like this story begins with a dame. This is my story that begins with a dame but I make no claims for its originality. Though I am a man composed of folios and phantasms, I often offer my services in a slightly more lucrative, more risqué—some might say a more *serious* occupation. I find lost people.

Usually the lost people don't want to be found. In Memphis, where I ply my strange vocation, there are many places to hide, places as dark as a thief's pocket: flash coves, buttocking shops and hot-water dosshouses. I am known in these places. I am respected in some, loathed in too many, welcome in few. Yet it is where I know to go. My name is Charlie Main.

I have a small office over Club Millar on Beale Street. The sign on my door says only "Charlie Main." I rely mostly on word-of-mouth business. Across the street from my office is the office of the recently deceased Mr. Honeywood Partridge, an extraordinary photographer: inside his office/gallery history crouches, gray and cold: the walls are festooned with iconic images of Dr. King, the Civil Rights marchers, Elvis, Sam Cooke. He was also, possibly, an FBI informer in the brutal conflicts of the 1960s. *C'est la guerre.* My associate, Anna Ford, says Mr. Partridge never pigeoned on anyone who didn't need pigeoning on. I don't care. But I do trust Anna the way an animal trainer trusts his luck. She's smart; she's got head-splatter to spare. She's as cunning as Becky Sharp. And she's made of fine parts which are put together well.

The dame (ahem—my new client) arrived one Friday morning just after I got to the office. My head was still full of *Laughter in the Dark,* the Nabokov novel I reluctantly left behind to assume my professional stance, one that required an office with my name on the door and an associate who is a wet dream's wet dream. Anna was gone that week. I was not sure where. She might have been working in disguise at one of the clubs, emporia of blues and blue tape. She did this occasionally because she said she could drum up business. I think she did it so she could take strangers home and show them the inside of her clothes. Anna liked, equally, the shine of bar lighting in a shot glass of whiskey (a glister of fish-hooks, she called it) and moral depravity. Hell, it wouldn't be wrong to say I loved her.

So, when a tentative knock arrived I shouted from behind my desk, "Come on in," in a voice meant to discourage the time-wasters, the feebs, the people whose fifteen-year-old tabby named Cuddles was AWOL.

She entered with an air. The air smelled like honeysuckle. She looked like a well-made dresser with all the drawers full. She was about five foot nine in her bare feet (later), had hair the color of tobacco and the kind of mouth that makes men want to drink there. She had skin the color of the Bosco I drank in short pants. She smiled like a kitten. A kitten with teeth like filed steel.

"Mr. Main?" she said. Her voice was made of a parasite's silk.

It was a good enough way to begin.

"How can I help you?" I countered.

"I was told." She stopped. She looked around like an actress in a melodrama. I waited. I'd done this interview before.

"I was told you find missing people." She finished with a silvery period on the end of her statement. It could have been plate silver or something finer.

"I try. That is what I get paid for. Trying."

She looked at me with a schoolteacher's moue.

"I hear you're better than that." She let the tip of her tongue dot her eyes.

"Thank you, Ms....?"

"Himes. Greta Himes."

"Pleased to meet you, Ms. Himes. Sit."

She folded herself downward. It was worth watching.

"Do you know a piano player named Blue Positive?"

"Heard of him. Plays at Smith Wigglesworth's place, right?"

"Sometimes he does. He used to, I should say."

"Until?"

"About ten days ago. He never showed up. Mr. Wigglesworth called me a week ago to ask his whereabouts and I couldn't imagine. I hadn't seen him in all that time but that's not unusual. He was, is, a tomcat. I waited a few more days before coming to you."

"I see. And this piano man, what is he to you?"

"My lover, Mr. Main. Nothing more, really. He and I sleep together when it's convenient."

"I appreciate your honesty. I'll give it a go. $500 a day plus expenses."

She didn't even hesitate. This began to interest me. She peeled off five C-notes and set them on my desk, right next to my baseball signed by Luis Aparicio.

"Gimme his addresses and friends' names and addresses and anything else you can think of and I'll get on it."

"I assumed everything was done online these days," she said, with a slight snark on the edge of her purr.

"If it were, you could find Mr. Blue," I said back. Not for the first time.

"You're right, of course." She stood, and I almost asked her to do it a few more times. She had a body that was full of poetry and terror.

I gave her my card, and she said she would e-mail me everything she could think of that might help. I thanked her and then tried to memorize the music she made walking away.

*

Of course, I did go online to find out everything I could about Blue Positive. And about Greta Himes.

Blue Positive, age 43, had learned to play blues piano with some of the greats. He was precocious and was sitting in with Furry Lewis when Blue was only twelve. He played the Delta circuit for a while but, about five years ago, decided he wanted to settle down and took a semi-permanent gig on Beale Street, where he became a popular attraction, both for his amazing left hand and his gold-toothed grin. He was playsome and randy (well-schooled in petticoats was Blue) and the stories of the beautiful women he bedded made me squirm. It had been a while. Where is Anna? I asked myself.

So Blue was established, even cut some records on the Madjack Label, was nominated for a Handy Award two years ago. There the biographical trail stopped. I could find nothing about Blue Positive that wasn't dated over a year ago.

Greta Himes proved as appealing, perhaps more so. She was born with a silver spoon in her wanton mouth to a Collierville, Tennessee, family, whose residence there went back hundreds of years. The name Himes meant money, prestige, banking, big business and Cayman Islands savings accounts. Greta's father, Grip Himes, married Cornelia Bryson in 1945. Cornelia was a singer and as black as Miles Davis. Needless to say, this caused great consternation in the Himes family, who were white as diatomaceous earth. They had two daughters: Camille, who went to Vassar and became a successful writer of murder mysteries before her tragic death in a freak boating accident, and Greta, who became nothing much at all except the rich, mulatto daughter of a prominent and powerful family.

These were fascinating histories. It was easy to see why Greta Himes gravitated toward Blue Positive and equally easy to see why Blue Positive wouldn't mind spending some of the

Himes family money, and, presumably, spending some sack time with that supernal body.

So why had he gone missing? It would seem he had landed in the lap of luxury. Who wouldn't want what he had?

I sat in front of the computer for another hour or so, randomly scrolling through pages about blues music, then pages about baseball, and then pages about Nabokov, and, in the end, pages with naked, attractive strangers rantum-scantum. That night I slept like a water-lily. I dreamed I was dead and seated at a dinner table with James Joyce, Brooks Robinson, Iris Murdoch and Greta Himes. Greta Himes was moving her fingers toward my tingling scrotum when the phone rang.

It was Greta Himes.

"I just sent you a list of names and addresses by e-mail."

"What time is it?" I was having trouble distinguishing the dream Greta from the voice on the phone.

"Eight in the a.m., bedhead," Greta said, with what I took for a coquettish lilt.

"Right. Thanks for the e-mail. I'll go look."

"Can we meet for lunch?" Greta now asked. Something was pear-shaped in the way she was approaching this caper.

"Um, yes, sure" I said, like the sharp I am. "B. B. King's okay?"

"Noon. I'll be there," Greta said.

And at noon there she was, almost lambent in the darkened restaurant, when I strolled in, print-out in hand. The list she had sent was extensive indeed. I was surprised not to see Mayor Wharton's name, or Steve Cohen's. Or the Pope's.

"You look tired," she said, half-rising.

"I'm fine. I need more coffee. I've been going over the list. It lacks—focus."

"I know. Once I got started I could not stop."

We ate some lunch. I had a lot of coffee. but it was Greta Himes who seemed jangled. She talked like an undammed river, mostly about inconsequential matters.

With dessert came this question: "Where do you wanna start?"

"I've an idea or two."

"Let's go, then."

"Wait. Ms. Himes. Wait. I don't work with anyone." (I didn't want to go into the whole Anna Ford thing.) Clients don't tag along."

"Oh." She seemed genuinely disappointed, like a spoiled child who just lost her inheritance. This lasted for a couple beats. "Will you see me home, then?"

Her home was off Parkway. It was the size of the Taj Mahal if the Taj Mahal were a rest stop. She invited me in and, damn it, I went. She was wearing this dress. It was made of butterfly wings. The sun shimmered through it. I am only human.

One of her domestics brought us coffee in the living room. It was a modest room. So is the Winter Palace. The couch on which we sat was the size of a small pasture, but softer.

After the manservant left us Greta Himes took off her shoes. There were her bare feet, dark like supple leather. They were the sexiest bare feet I'd ever seen. She tucked them under herself the way women do. I missed them immediately.

"Get comfortable," she said.

"What are we doing?" I asked. It was part of the training.

She looked at me like I had invented Swift Peter, the mythical Cooper-Young beast that white merchants used to scare blacks out of the neighborhood. Her perfect face was squinched perfectly.

"You're funny," she said. She pulled her dress up over her knees, with a practiced nonchalance. Her thighs were bronze. I was defeated.

In her bedroom she undid my every button and catch slowly, both of us standing and swaying next to her vast bed. My knees were as weak as a bled calf's. When I was down to my hector protector she smiled at the bulge and touched it with the tip of her manicured pinkie. I imagine this is the classy way to approve a dick.

Then she let her dress fall. Then she undid her bra. Then she let her thin black panties slither down her magnificent gams. Her pubic hair, a glorious map of Tasmania, against her coffee-colored skin was as black as Alaskan sealskin.

She knelt and pulled my pistol out of its holster. She palmed it for a few agonizing minutes and then took it past her bright red lips into the warm pocket of her cheeks. Soon, I got the idea. Soon, we were in bed and she was sitting on me and riding me as if I were the Scrambler at the Mid-South Fair, (gone now, too). It was quite a performance. I was good. She was better. After it was over she mewed like a kitten.

"Find my Blue for me, Mr. Dick," she said, and tittered at her own joke.

"I aim to, Ms. Himes. I aim to start just as soon as I know my legs still work."

"You're funny," she said for the second time. "And please call me Greta."

*

I didn't understand what had happened but I didn't care. We both itched. I thought of it like that. And now I was back on the case, professional from the brim of my porkpie roofer to the aching culty-gun of my well-used body.

I started at the last place Blue Positive played, Smith Wigglesworth's. I knew Smith from the old days. We had gone to East High together. Smith played tight end. I played the fool. We were acquaintances back then and, since we both worked on Beale, we got together occasionally for lunch. By the time I got to his place they were unstacking chairs and cleaning glasses, getting ready for the evening's crowd. I was shown into Smith's office.

His athlete's body had gone to seed, but hell, we all weighed a bit more, and we all still thought we were as beautiful as teenagers. Smith wore a suit out of some material that looked like a cross between linen and tin foil. It gleamed.

"Charlie Main," Smith said, not rising and not taking his eyes off the computer screen in front of him. "Too late for lunch, my man. Did we have a lunch date today that I forgot?" Now he raised his Paul Newman eyes and brushed back his shoulder-length silver hair.

"No, this is business, Smith. We can do lunch another day."

"Mr. Serious. Tell me about it."

"I'm looking for Blue Positive."

"Who isn't?" he said, his eyes went back to the screen and then back to mine. Was he uncomfortable suddenly?

"Yes, but I am being paid to do it."

"Difference noted."

"You got any ideas?"

"You checked The Castle of Missing Men? Gamblers and drinkers go in but they do not come out." He couldn't resist a tight smile.

"You got any ideas?" Sometimes repeating questions works. I don't know why.

"Nah," he said as if he thought I might let him go at that.

"Come on, Smith. We understand each other. You know something."

"Not much, Chuck, not much." He was the only person who called me Chuck. I hated it.

"When did you see him last?"

"Last night he worked. Um, this is the 24th. Musta been July 14, 15."

"Anything special happen that night?"

Here Smith stopped. He pushed himself away from the computer. He leaned back in his leather desk chair.

"Maybe," he said. His eyes, the color of pulled pork, were doing that funny thing again. They were positively hiding something, trying to look inside their owner to see if he should spill.

"Smith," I said, letting the exasperation show.

"Big white guy came in. Big. I mean like Secret Service big. Looked like he could take you out while singing "Rockin' Robin," and never miss a beat. Like a walking wall. Solemn dude, asked my man Petey where Blue was. Blue was on break and in the back. Big guy went back there as if he had permission from Hitler himself. In the back room I don't know what happened. The big white guy left after about five minutes, walked right by me, giving me the smartass grin, like he might enjoy eating my gonads for breakfast. That's it."

"Blue never came back out?"

"No, he came out, finished his set. Seemed a little shaky maybe, not much. Blue was an interior sorta guy, you know? He finished his set. But he never came back. I tried his apartment numerous times. Sent Petey around to see if he was at home. Petey said the place looked untouched but there was no Mr. Positive."

"Petey went in?"

"Well, heh-heh, yeah. He did. I gave him a little shiv, you know, a little skeleton key."

"Okay. Thanks, Smith. I get the picture."

"You need Blue's address?" Smith now said. He seemed relieved I was going.

"Got it," I called back over my shoulder.

Blue Positive lived in the Akimbo Arms, an apartment complex just off Beale, a stone's throw from FedEx Forum, the AA somehow surviving when they razed or gentrified everything within walking distance of the mammoth NBA mushroom.

As I ambled down the western end of Beale I passed the usual buskers and cackleberries, a bum-simple beggar, a Creole Conjurewoman. Ah, Beale, still the American Dream forced through a squeezebox and spat out, multihued and wet with dribble.

The guy who ran Akimbo Arms was a pipsqueak named Pipsqueak Martin. He used to be a mob marker but emphysema had slowed him down some.

"Charlie Main," he said, coming from around his desk to take my hand. "Hot enough for you?" I recognized this as a standard greeting in Memphis, something like "Howdy" for a Texan.

"Looking for Blue Positive," I told him straight out. I didn't really want chitchat with Pipsqueak Martin.

"That's a mystery, ain't it? Mystery inside of an enema, as they say. Ain't seen him, Charlie."

"Can I look around his apartment?"

"Sure," he said, after acting like he was thinking it over. "Let the po po see it, why not my old pal, Charlie Main? You're one upscale busy, my friend. You're one of the good guys. You know Pipsqueak's got the bull horrors."

"Law been here already?"

"Yeah, yesterday it was."

Pipsqueak let me in and then let me alone. I closed the door behind me and locked it. Blue's apartment was as neat as the altar of a church. Bed, dresser, computer, keyboards, stereo and the largest selection of jazz records I have ever seen. 33s and 78s. Like Crumb's house, all categorized and in original covers. Impressive. Of course all I wanted to do was look at his computer. I turned it on. Maybe he was careless with passwords. Maybe he didn't clear history. Maybe his screensaver said *"I have absquatulated to New Orleans."* It was a prayer, really. Nothing is ever that easy.

The computer was clean or had been wiped clean. He used Google Chrome. That's about the extent of the information I got off it. If Anna were around, damn her, she could get me in. She never saw a hard drive she couldn't cozy up to.

I ran my hand underneath the desk surface and found fuckle. I stood and looked around the immaculate room. There is nothing for me here, I thought. I looked at his clothes closet. Hipster jazzman-wear. Nice stuff. Then I saw it. There was a military style jacket on a satin-padded hanger, the kind that was popular after Sergeant Pepper taught the band to play. I took it off its hanger and ran my hand over the brightly colored tunic. Tucked under one of the epaulettes, seemingly a part of the design, was a coral-pink zip drive about the size of a lot lizard's polished nail. I was about to try it in Blue's computer when Pipsqueak opened the door.

"How's it going, Charlie?" he said, sticking his weasel head inside.

I slipped the zip drive into my pants pocket.

"Nothing here," I said and brushed past him.

"Told you so," he said.

He hadn't but that didn't matter.

I made it to my office in record time. The door to Mr. Partridge's studio had a large sign in its window saying "Closed for Maintenance." I felt I had something vital in my pocket and when I pulled up the files on the zip I discovered I was right. I had something. Something good. Something I hated and wished I didn't have.

*

On the North side of Beale, closer to Big Muddy, there was a three-story nondescript edifice. It held a real-estate office, a lawyer's office and some charity connected to the Memphis Grizzlies. It also held a small office on the third floor, down a dim hallway far away from the other businesses. On its door it said, in recently painted calligraphy, "Harris P. Kayshun, Accountant."

I opened the door without knocking. A woman who resembled the TV actress Kristin Chenoweth sprang from her chair. She was stuck somewhere between shock and indignation. It was clear people didn't just walk in to see Harris P. Kayshun. It was also clear that he was no accountant.

"Can I help you?" she practically snarled.

"Get Mr. Kayshun for me," I said. I tried to sound like Philip Marlowe. I was afraid of Harris P. Kayshun, and for good reason. His connections had connections.

"He's not here. He's in St. Louis."

"He's here," I insisted. "Tell him it's Mr. Blue." I sat down in the room's only chair not behind her desk.

She appeared flustered for a moment and then she opened the door behind her desk and disappeared. I looked at the office. It was cheap, temporary, perfunctory. The pictures on the walls could have come from any Days Inn.

She returned. Her smile was as practiced as "Feelin' all right."

"I don't know who you are, but Mr. Kayshun said he had five minutes."

I let her have her attitude. I walked past her into the office of Harris. P. Kayshun. He was standing next to his desk. He wore a suit that cost more than my car. It was out of place in his shabby office. Even his desk was cheap. He was about six two and looked like he could handle himself. And me.

"Who are you, sir?" Harris spoke.

"A guy with some questions about Positive Blue."

"Positive ..." he began.

"Can it," I said. "I am in possession of numerous e-mails and documents between you and Mr. Blue. They may very well put you in hot water. They may very well make a strong case for your going to jail."

I was partly bluffing. The computer files consisted of pages and pages of correspondence between Blue Positive and Harris P. Kayshun and they pointed toward some kind of nefarious deal (or deals) but they were not more specific than that. Kayshun had been funneling a lot of bees and honey into Blue's accounts, especially right before the piano man disappeared.

The door opened. A man who was made of whatever they make fireplugs out of entered. He stood by the door. His silence was like suffocation. I tried to take a deep breath. I was playing a weak hand and, perhaps, playing it badly.

"You have nothing of the sort," Kayshun said. "What do you want, Mr. ...?"

"Main," I said. "Charlie Main."

"Private peon."

"That's right. Hired to find Blue Positive."

Kayshun sat down behind his desk. He nodded at the roughneck, who went back outside. He played with a Shane Battier bobblehead on his desk. He took a deep breath and beamed like Barabbas.

"What you have, Mr. Main, Charlie, could embarrass me, it's true. It, however, is not the Pandora's box you think it is. I am willing to pay for its return: for good faith, you might say."

"How much?" Why not?

"Would 50,000 sound right?"

He was darling. He was real loveable.

"You know it sounds right," I said. "I'll take it. As long as the whereabouts of Blue Positive are thrown in to sweeten the pot."

He smiled a grim smile.

"Mr. Positive," he said almost dreamily. Almost the way a lover would say it.

"I can't," he said.

"Okay," I said, and started to rise.

"Mr. Main," he said quickly. "What will you do with Blue? Will you send him away?"

"I have no intention of doing anything with Mr. Blue except telling my client where he is."

He seemed to think this over.

"Okay," he said.

*

I called Greta Himes. I told her I knew where her boyfriend was.

"Mr. Main," she cooed. "You are wonderful. I don't know how to repay you."

"Yes, you do," I said.

"Cheeky," she said in that voice that turned men into goats.

"I'll tell you where he is and I'll send you the bill."

"Mr. Business," she said. "Are you sure...?"

I wasn't.

"Yes," I said.

And then I told her and then I sat behind my desk with $50,000 dollars in the locked drawer where I usually kept my blunt, and I created an invoice and e-mailed it to her. I sat back and tried to feel good about myself. It wouldn't happen. Something was wrong. I felt it in Kayshun's office and I felt it when I talked to Greta Himes.

I slept badly that night. And when I woke I still had a bad feeling in my gut.

I went to the office but I didn't want to see anyone.

Then the Creole Conjurewoman entered, a diddykay of colorful rags and trinkets. She was dusky and glittery at the same time, like a night when the clouds are torn newspaper and the moon a buttery nightlight.

"Hi," I said. "I'm closed."

She fixed me with her one eye that was not occluded by cloud.

"Open for a poor conjurewoman, Mr. Main?" she asked in a voice like a giraffe's tongue.

"No, I, I'm not open, Ma'am. Sorry."

"Not even if I know who killed Blue Positive."

I involuntarily stood up. I wanted to hit her. I wanted to hit myself. My head swam. Her expression never changed. She looked like Maria Ouspenskaya on a bad day. I sat back down. She sat on the chair on the other side of the desk and her back was so bent it looked as if she was about to teeter out of it.

"Wake you up, did it?"

"Please," I said. I don't know what I was asking.

"Not to worry, Mr. Main. You get to keep the fifty thousand."

"Who are you?" It was worth asking.

"Conjurewoman. You know me. All over. You've seen."

I hadn't but I played along.

"Blue Positive is dead?"

"As dead as Vladimir Nabokov," she said. She grinned like a wolf. She knew too much.

"How?"

"Shot through the heart. Twice. Both times through the heart. Nice clean kill, yes?"

"I don't understand. How did this happen?"

"You led her to him." Now she didn't seem so funny. Her voice dropped an octave. I imagined she could be mean as a nightmare given the chance.

I started to shake.

"G-Greta?" I said, weakly.

"Halfbreed bitch. Of course Greta."

"But why?"

"Two reasons. Jealousy, and she was paid to do it."

"She didn't need money," I said. I was playing with a blank deck.

"She was in a bad way. Her father was threatening to take the house, her car, her servants. He wanted her gone, out of Memphis. He was brokering a big deal and afraid having a mixed-race daughter might queer it. Kayshun somehow dealt himself into the deal."

"Kayshun?" But I knew. It had to come back to Kayshun.

"You had a part in this sordid affair, Mr. Main, but don't take it hard. It wasn't personal. You were used, but it could have been someone else."

"I don't understand."

"Look," she said. Her voice did not seem as raspy. "Blue Positive was a gunsel. Hired talent. But he was also as gay as Liberace. And he was Kayshun's bum boy, as well as one of his operatives. You dig?"

"I don't know." I put my face in my hands.

"And Greta Himes?" I asked.

"She was really Blue's lover. She was mad for him, if a woman with the morals of a dingo can be mad for anyone. When Blue did a Judge Crater she genuinely wanted him back. She loved him—in her way."

"She knew Kayshun knew where he was?'

"That's right. She also knew he would never tell her. He wanted the boy for himself. We might give Mr. Kayshun at least that much credit. He loved Blue, too. Still, he was ready to do what he had to do, like the good Joe Bonanno he is. Blue became expendable when you started digging in the service of that wildcat. How whimsical for Kayshun to use her as the instrument of Blue's demise."

"And the big deal?"

"I'm not sure. I think Kayshun might have cut out the father. He certainly made sure the daughter became his to utilize."

"Jesus," I said. "And I led her to Blue. I did it. His blood is on my hands."

"Don't feel so bad about it. Some folks need killing."

I looked up. Her gypsy voice was suddenly as smooth as Ruby Wilson's.

"What did Blue Positive do to need killing?"

"He killed Honeywood Partridge."

Now I stood up. My eyes popped. I was a cartoon gull. I didn't know anything about anything.

"Mr. Partridge died of a stroke."

"Complications from a stroke, yes. That's what they said."

"But—"

"He was killed before the FBI stuff leaked out. There are things in Mr. Partridge's file that could upset some official applecart."

"The Feds had him killed?"

"Who knows? But whoever was behind it paid Blue Positive to kill Mr. Partridge and make it look like a medical anomaly."

"And they got to Blue through Kayshun."

"Yes."

"Damn them all to hell. Let's go get Kayshun."

"Gone, brother. Gone like Jackie Brenston. Gone like Roscoe Gordon."

"Dead?"

"Oh no. Just—*pfft*. Disappeared."

"Fuck."

"Frustrating, isn't it? They did get Greta Himes though. Caught her on the scene, beautiful little silver beader still smoking."

"The Feds. The mob. Gunsel piano players. Deadly dames. What is going on?"

"Life, baby, just life."

"I don't want any part of it."

The old crone put a hand over mine. Her hand was as soft as cream. "Can't get away from life, sugar."

I looked up into her eyes. Her eye.

"You slept with that mulatto, didn't you?" she said. It wasn't the conjurewoman's voice anymore. It was Anna Ford's.

I was through with histrionic surprise. I was as tired at Tiresias.

"Damn you, Anna," I said. This time I rose with righteous dudgeon.

She gave a graveyard chuckle and began dismantling her complex disguise. Soon, except for some greasepaint, some tacky maquillage and random streaks in her hair where the jasey had stuck, my associate sat before me, stripped to her underwear.

I sat back down. I was too dazed for rage.

"Oh, and I got you this." She reached into the conjurewoman's bag and pulled out a book wrapped in a plastic bag.

"It's a first of *Pale Fire*. Signed."

A book about as rare, as we say, as a John Calipari fan in Memphis.

"Jesus, Anna, this must have cost you a mint."

"We can afford it now," she said.

She stood up and walked around the desk. She unhooked her bra. Her breasts were as full as a vicar's wisdom. I thought I heard the music of the spheres but it might have been Howlin' Wolf.

For a while we forgot about the world. For a while we did things humans do to assuage loss and to express feelings too deep for words alone. For a while there never was a piano player named Blue Positive, nor a chocolaty temptress named Greta Himes.

Then I kissed Anna's hot mouth long and hard.

"You were here the whole time?"

"Right behind you, every step."

"You're amazing, Anna Ford."

"I know, Charlie Main."

"I didn't really sleep with her."

How good was her knowledge of the whole miserable kerfluffle?

"Sure, Bunky," she said. "Sure."

ALAN'S APPROACH

Alan stepped from the shadows just as she was passing. He didn't mean for it to begin this way. He didn't mean to be in the shadows.

Perhaps Alan, poor gowk, was guilty of overthinking this whole thing. Perhaps what was called for was a more temperate approach, a card, sent anonymously, with a stamp affixed upside down, which Alan thought meant "sealed with a kiss."

No, not a kiss. It could not begin with even the suggestion of a kiss. Alan fretted. Late into the white nights he sat beneath his desk lamp and tried to focus. He pressed his fingers against his forehead as if he could force the insula to react.

He didn't mean to step from the shadows. She was so lovely. He saw her walking down the sidewalk just as carefree as a child at play, as if she were unaware that she was moonquakes and arrhythmia. She looked a bit like the actress Patsy Kensit.

Alan stepped from the shadows just as she was passing.

"I won't hurt you if you don't move," he said.

It was not what he had prepared. Alan was adlibbing.

BLUNGE

"The false or substituted bride is one of the most widespread of all folktale motifs."
>   —from *Funk & Wagnall's Standard Dictionary of Folklore, Mythology, and Legend*

I never noticed before. My wife is left-handed. This gives me pause as I stand in the doorway, a mixer dripping with cake batter in my hand. She's always been so loving, with the kids and all.

On TV there is a nature show, the kind of thing she likes, one predator on top of another. I watch her watch for a few minutes. One drip falls from my blades and, in slow motion, careens floorward. It lands and there is that frozen moment, an explosion.

Somewhere in the farthest corners of the house I can hear the muffled sounds of our children, lost in their own worlds, lost to us.

My wife turns toward me and sees me standing there. The terror in her face is worth the forfeited time, the mess. I return to the kitchen, a different man. I am armed now. There will be no more secrets, no more surprises from here on out, from the middle of my life till the final reconsideration.

THE HISTORY OF
LUNGFISH MELODY

In the dusty light of nearnight he plugs the last word in and it's done, a first book. He sits and stares at it as if it may come to life in front of him, wriggle off the desk and drop to the floor to scurry under furniture or worse out the door. He likes the name, emboldened and larger-fonted: **Lungfish Melody**. He says it over and over to himself like a pop ditty stuck in the mind, a snag of lyric like "Cry Me a River."

When he puts it into the mailbox it doesn't quite fit and he has to angle it slightly, a child bending its head down so you can nail the crate shut. The address looks as if it could be any address, a random house. But his label affixed to the upper left corner spells out his name and residence as clearly as the peal of matins, the peel left over. Will it find its way back here, along a breadcrumb route? Will it need to?

Did he remember phone number, e-mail, alternate address? Did he put return postage on the return postage place? He begins to sweat. His heart pounds like a nine-pound hammer and the sun has never been this hot before, mean as a swinked gypsy, bearing down on him, baring its teeth, bearing ill will.

It's not worth it. Nothing could be worth this. What if he receives a call from their solicitor? He can be sued for his words. He's heard tell of it. Writers with books burned, names dragged through the mud, dragged into a courtroom to defend their right to say such things, to say anything.

He doesn't want it published or even read. He was a fool to send it to strangers. **Lungfish Melody**, what could be worse? Everyone is stranger, his life is out there on the line, his lines hanging up, words without meaning. He only wants it back, his book, his life. He takes it all back. He'll never write again. He is sorry. Lawks, he is so fucking sorry.

Corey Mesler

ROCK PASTE

When I was a child, a small child, a boy, I wanted to make rock paste. This was really just part of my overall experimentalism, my personal belief system that considered the world a place ripe for change, for alchemy. In my backyard I was a prince, a scientist-prince. This made up for the more public front yard where I was not quite so welcome, where I was called sissy and little girl and worse. But, on the 25-foot cement patio in my back yard on Kenneth Street, I was Curie, Pasteur, Einstein. Like most boys my age, at this particular time in the 1960s, I had a chemistry set. With it I could make no experiment work. This was probably because I mixed those colorful powders willy-nilly, with no guide. Reading the instructions was for more prosaic minds. And I really believed that I would stumble upon some combination that would engender something miraculous. Wasn't this the way x-rays were invented, by accident? Yes, I saw it on John Nesbitt's *Passing Parade*. I really didn't see my complete ignorance of science as a drawback. I wanted to roll God's dice anyway.

Anyway, I had a theory. My theory said that if I could pound the rocks and stones that I found in the yard, where

144

they were abundant, pound them hard enough with a ball-peen hammer, steadily enough, I could pulverize them (the operative word here is *pulverize*) and produce a powder so fine that, when mixed with tap water, I would have rock paste. A paste made from rock dust. This seemed to me one of the finest ideas I had had up to that point in my young life.

I took my handful of stones and my hammer and sat on the patio near the faucet. It seemed to be important to be near my water source, as if, perhaps, I might have to add the water quickly before the rock dust changed back to rock. I began to pound on the stones, using the pavement as my mortar, one of my dad's hammers as pestle. The initial smashing was satisfying. The colorful rocks, as they crumbled, seemed to me to be the very building blocks of the Earth. And I was Lord of it.

But, soon friends, my girlish wrist grew tired. Very soon it grew tired. I looked at what I had crushed. It was far from fine. It was really just rock crumbles. I put a cupped handful of water into a plastic pail and added what I had crushed so far. It just looked silly. It was wet gravel. Wet gravel did not seem a particularly satisfying result to my experiment. And, here I confess: I have never really conducted a successful experiment. Through laziness, lack of focus, and just plain lack of knowledge, I could make nothing from nothing. I was no alchemist. I am no alchemist.

In college, after five years of mostly English and Philosophy classes, I was called into my advisor's office. It was there suggested that if a degree I sought I had better take something other than English classes, namely the required Phys Ed, a language, biology and zoology. I thanked my advisor for his wisdom and insight and shook his hand. I then went home and told my parents that I was through with college. They were disappointed of course. I wanted to tell them that I had made wet gravel instead of rock paste, but, what I really said was, I am going to be a bookseller and writer.

And this is what I became. My experiment with my own life is not finished yet but it's a safe bet I will no longer pursue the breaking apart of raw materials to try and affect some sort of magical, elemental change. I will only do this metaphorically, on the dreamy page, in my dreamy head. And, in experiments done metaphorically, friends, there are few who know what fails and what doesn't.

LUDA CHRIST

Jesus' brother Luda was something of a tartar in concert, a dement. He was grouchy, he was confrontational, he was taciturn. He showed his back to the audience when he played solos. He told his bass player, Micah Rejoyce, that he was tired of playing the standards.

"I wanna do something—outré," he would say. "Something renegade. If I have to sing "He walks with me and he talks with me" one more time I'm gonna rip my own head off."

Luda's band, Bacchanal, stayed with him, even as he began drifting into uncharted waters.

Eventually, of course, he got his wish. His recording of "Old Rugged Cross" in 9/8 time reinvented jazz. His later club dates, after the whole resurrection thing with his brother blew over, revealed a musician ahead of his time, a risk-taker, maybe the first of what would come to be known as the avant garde. Luda blew sax as if ten horns were in his head.

Daniel, writing in *DownBeat*, said, "And the great horn that is between his eyes is the first king."

The *Jerusalem Times* said of his album, *Luda Way Out*, "His horn shall be exalted with honor."

The accolades continue to this day. His version of "A Love Supreme" rivals its author's. And when he sat in with Gabriel "Gabe" Clooney and his Big Band, he brought himself a whole new audience, a younger set of worshipers.

Chauncy "Lord" Westbrook said of Luda: "He was the best of us, really. A heavy cat with a lot of baggage, you dig? Where he came from, man, I don't know, I just think he had that whole family thing, and that was a tough hood to come from, right? I don't know. His brother gettin lynched—what can you say? Those were his times. Can I have a hit of that?"

And on and on.

When Luda disappeared there were some who said it was the same cabal responsible for his brother's woes. Some said it was Old Scratch come to collect a debt. (There is some confusion here with Old Scratch Records, which had released, in 1982, a pirated edition of a live performance by Bacchanal.) Suffice it to say Luda was gone, real gone. He left behind only his heavenly music. Of the man, really, we know little. But we can still put on "Which I Commanded" or "Crosswalk" and be sanctified.

Let Luda's own words be his epitaph: "I only wanted to take music as far as I could. Or put another way, have music take me as far as it could. I let the notes lead me to the Promised Land, you folla? I been to the Promised Land, man, and it's just another club. Just another stop on the circuit. Ye followers, I say unto thee. Jazz is only one path but it's a sweet one. And, finally, where I go ye cannot follow. As Billie said, 'Don't threaten me with love, baby. Let's just go walking in the rain'."

BUCKY BUSTARD

He came to us from Spain.

It could have been the New Hebrides, or even the Old Hebrides. It could have been Far Tortuga, or Near Tortuga. But it wasn't. It was Spain. That was exotic enough.

We were unsophisticated suburban kids, middle to lower-middle class, and the school we attended, Nicholas Blackwell High School, had just gone through bussing. We were in flux. We were growing up in the early 1970s, a time between times. In Memphis we were just seeing our first hippies. We were learning about pot and sex and hygiene. The latter two were taught to us by one of the football coaches. God help us.

And we were enjoying our time, most of us, in the early 1970s. We were experimenting with new ways to dress, new music, new ways of being. Some of us were struggling with the race thing. We were only a few years removed from the assassination of Martin Luther King, Jr., in our own city. We heard adults say, "It's good they got him." And many of us were aware of how ugly that was, how backward. Some of us did not care.

It was high school. It was a skimble-skamble glomeration. It was a labyrinth with a centaur and no thread. The only thread we had, perhaps, was our shared mystification.

So we drifted in and out of each other's lives. Friendships formed during evenings at Trish's house or Christy's, over junk food and King Crimson, Fever Tree, The Doors, The Mothers of Invention, and The Beatles. Over hearts and dominoes. We didn't know it was a liminal time for us. We didn't know that this closeness would not last. We were young and free and horny and full of ourselves.

We didn't know what we didn't know.

Then it happened. Change, even if small. A throb of divergence.

Into our midst came the Bustard family, direct from Spain. There seemed to be a dozen kids, though there were only four. I think four. Suddenly they were among us and were the most popular topic of our confabs. Suddenly Mrs. Bustard had organized a school tennis team, a rare enough thing at that time. Some of my friends joined the team, even if it meant picking up a racquet for the first time. Mrs. Bustard was an inspiring teacher, almost a mage of the game. Some lovely lasses began to play the game. They looked like burnished copper in their short white skirts. Even I began to play, though I did not attempt to join the team. I was like an emu on skates. I was not fluid, or sporty, or strong. But I wanted to belong. You see that, right?

And the center of this stir was the oldest son, named Francis, called Bucky. He was tall and well-built and athletic and as handsome as a chevalier. He had shoulder-length blond hair which he wore sometimes in a ponytail. He had cheekbones you could cut cheese on. And when he sat on the basketball team's bench he crossed one leg over the other, like a girl. It was European. It was sexy. He was also the star of his mother's tennis team. He was too much to take in all at once. We all loved him. We all wanted to befriend him.

So, of course, he got the princess. It's that kind of story. And, though there were many, many fetching young women in our high school, there was only one princess. Her name was Lita. Her name still is Lita. And she was everything Bucky was: beautiful, smart, talented, kind, funny and athletic. It was as if she had spent her high school years waiting for him. In this fairy tale we shall say that she had.

Because Lita and I had known each other since fourth grade—I had seen her through many boyfriends, some my best friends, never to be considered a suitor myself—I was somewhat thrown into Bucky's orbit. Plus, his family had moved onto Bluefield Street, just three blocks from my family's house on Kenneth Street. I ended up playing driveway basketball at the Bustard's. I ended up sharing Thai stick and fireworks with them, one memorable 4th of July. So I knew Bucky, and yet, I didn't. I didn't have the sang-froid, or the confidence, to chat with him alone, or over extended periods of time. We were friendly, though not friends. That's it.

So the prince and princess walked our halls, resplendent, shimmering, untouchable, yet somehow *ours*. It made us happy to see them together. It made us jealous. It turned us on, like small humming appliances, like alley cats.

Meanwhile, I had a girlfriend of my own, a buxom junior, who was as sexy as a flame and who took my virginity. Well, to say she took it implies, perhaps, that I was not willing to give it. I was. Eager, hungry, vertiginous with lust. She and I spent many nights wrestling on her father's couch. It was the year of hotpants and that fashion fad was a spur, a green light if in name only. Needless to say, it was a heady time for me. Sex was all I thought about. Somehow I passed my classes, smoked dope, won the vice-presidency of our senior class, hung out at Trish's. But all the time, I only wanted to have more sex.

My girlfriend and I had some rocky times. We broke up. We got back together for the physical pleasures. We broke up again. This went on for most of my senior year. Meanwhile, there were cracks in the glittering façade of the prince and princess. Things weren't going well. I didn't ever learn why. By the time we graduated, Lita had tied a can to Bucky and set him loose. Soon afterwards she announced she was attending college out of town. Our lives were splintering.

And, on the night of my high school graduation, my girlfriend was across town cuckolding me with my best friend. This best friend tried to score with all my girlfriends, and with her he succeeded. *C'est la guerre.*

The summer between high school and college was a sinsemilla miasma for me. My friend Mike had a red convertible, and we spent every single day riding around in it, playing tennis, looking for women, and smoking copious amounts of locoweed. I was tanned and at a level of fitness I would never again enjoy. And my blond curly hair fell to my shoulders *à la* Roger Daltrey. It was a golden summer.

In the fall I started at Memphis State, a journalism major (this would very quickly morph into an English major, as I had only recently discovered Literature with a capital L), and a naïf about the world of academics and, indeed, about the entire adult world. Stepping over that threshold after high school can be invigorating or it can scare the cats out of you. I was closer to the latter. The confidence I had in high school was leaching away. I became again what I was in childhood: afraid of life.

About this time a young woman swam into my ken. Not just any young woman, but the prettiest young woman I had ever seen (I still think that to this day). I saw her at McDonald's when

Mike and I were cruising. I saw her at sporting events (she went to Raleigh Egypt High School, which was our closest rival, our sibling school). Her name was Wendy. I believe her name still is Wendy.

I began to research her the way one did back then. I asked everyone about her. The news back was that she had a boyfriend but he was, perhaps, on the way out. I saw the boyfriend. He didn't deserve her. She was Aphrodite and Venus and Laura Petrie. She was dark like dark wood, short but beautifully shaped, like a fine piece of pottery. She was the daystar. I wanted her so bad it consumed me.

So I made bold. I don't know how I made bold. Some of my high-school tomcat ways were still with me. Some of my modest magic. I simply showed up on her doorstep one night. Her mother answered and I asked for Wendy and her mother, an older version of that sable beauty, showed me into the living room. A nice house, an economic step up from my family's. Her mother said "Wendy is doing her homework upstairs. Who should I say is calling?" I told her but added, "the name will mean nothing to her."

I don't remember what we talked about that first night. I was nervous but I was driven on by her magnificence. If anything, close up, she was even prettier. I simply explained to her that I had been mooning over her and would like the opportunity of a date. There was a fluster, a flutter, a change in the room's chemistry. Reader, she said yes.

I was gaga. I was a foolish swain. I was wearing my head as a seat cushion.

I knew little about Wendy. I thought someone had told me she played tennis. It was common ground. Tennis.

And, it so happened that my new school, Memphis State, had a tennis match upcoming with the University of Tennessee.

I knew this because the tennis coach at Memphis State at that time was the esteemed Tommy Buford, and I was taking tennis for my athletic credit. He recommended the class go see the team play Tennessee.

And, maybe you're ahead of me, but the star of the Tennessee team, I already knew, was our own Francis "Bucky" Bustard. He was returning to Memphis to play college tennis. It was perfect. It was an alignment of true things; it was kismet.

It was too good to be true. I now saw that our first date had to be the Memphis State-Tennessee tennis match. I thought this was a way to impress Wendy, to tell her about this god from Bartlett who was my friend, who was to tennis what Jim West was to government agents. I could build Bucky up, build up the match, make it all seem sparkly and unreal. It was gonna be the perfect first date.

I brought flowers. It was a nice touch. And it helped when I had to enter Wendy's home and meet her father and explain, briefly, who I was and how I knew Wendy. I don't remember what I said but he let me leave with his treasure. Wendy and I walked together out into the night.

She was so dishy. I was so smitten.

It was in October and the weather had turned windy and cold, colder than usual for this time of year in Memphis. I was nervous driving to Memphis State. I was nervous walking her to the tennis court. I kept looking at her, reminding myself that this was the woman I had been craving. She was made of chocolate and light.

We had to sit through a preliminary match before the main event, which would be the top-ranked players of each team playing each other. We couldn't talk much because it was tennis. I was cold and worried. I didn't think it was a good start. Wendy sat next to me with only a light sweater on. I wanted to take her back to my cave and build a fire and cover her with bison skins.

Then Bucky Bustard began to warm up. He was lithe and graceful and beautiful. He stroked the ball as if his movements were the exertion of immaculate gods. I brightened up. This was my friend, Bucky. Wendy must be impressed. Her face was inscrutable, like the face on an ancient coin.

The match began. The match was over before I could even register what happened. Bucky Bustard was beaten so cleanly, so easily, so quickly, that it was as if I were witnessing the assassination of JFK all over again. Our beautiful god! Our high school prince! Our perfect hero! He wasn't that great a tennis player. He was ordinary. And I was sorry I was there to witness him having his wings clipped.

I don't remember the rest of the date. It must have gone okay because Wendy and I saw each other for about three months. Three lovely months. I remember kissing her seemed like dreamland to me. I remember thinking I was in heaven. I was holding Wendy in my arms. My memories of those three months have been smudged on the blackboard inside my leaky bonce. I can only read a few phrases of pentimento: We went to a Steely Dan concert. We made plans to look into Transcendental Meditation, which was the rage at that time. We held hands. I remember so little else. I remember the night I cupped her teacup breast and she rebuffed me as quickly as Simon Peter cut the ear off the high priest's servant. It was not on. I saw it all as clearly as Merlin saw each tomorrow. I was to be a brief blip on Wendy's dating screen. She was not going to fall in love with me. Of course she wasn't.

Wendy was gone gone. She stepped off the Streetcar Named Desire and caught the bus that read "Further." I was dust. I was left tailed by a can. I was left holding the apple and I had only myself to blame for picking it.

There was a worm in the apple. I know that worm. I know that apple. I have lived outside the garden for years.

And what of Bucky Bustard? He disappeared. He left this earthly plane. I don't mean he died. I mean that the Bucky we made of glitter and paste, the one who briefly captured the heart of our princess, is no more. He is gone the way of all earthy gods. I wish I could talk to him now, though I probably would have little to say. I no longer believe.

LIVING WITH ANDERSON

While I was out Anderson rearranged the entire apartment. My
chair no longer sat in the corner facing the big-screen TV. My
chair now sat facing the picture window. And the big-screen TV
was in the hallway where watching it would be impractical, if not
impossible. In the kitchen the table rested on two legs, its surface
now used for tacking up drawings the nieces and nephews had
sent. In the icebox I found my shoes, the TV Guide, a beard
trimmer, a Matchbox car I had not seen since childhood, and some
important papers. The marriage certificate was not among them. I
later discovered it in the bathroom, underneath the clawfoot tub.
Anderson was nowhere to be found. With trepidation I walked
down the hall—now the TV room—toward the bedroom. I
passed the bathroom, where the aquarium sat on the toilet. The
bedroom door was closed. What would I find there? I wondered.
Perhaps no bed, perhaps pictures of Anderson's lovers instead
of the framed poem which once sat on the nightstand. Perhaps
all my power tools would be displayed on the credenza which we
had moved to the garage. Perhaps Anderson herself would be
there, but changed, changed utterly, a new Anderson with lighter
hair, tattoos and a figure more zaftig than previously imagined.

Perhaps, and this was my greatest fear, the room would be empty as if no one had ever lived there, the wall down to pasteboard, the floor unpolished wood. The bedroom door was closed. I stood a long time outside it. I was relieved the door was closed and that Anderson was not at home. I would make these discoveries myself. I would face them and they would become part of me and I would be an agent of change, also, rather than its cat's-paw. I raised my fist to knock on the bedroom door. What if a stranger were inside? Right before I knocked I heard Anderson's key in the apartment door. I turned toward the sound. When she entered she would not be able to see me. I could decide not to answer her inquiring call of my name. Would she call my name? I could enter the bedroom and disappear and she would be the one left querulous and dazed. I knew what to do. Just as I put my hand on the bedroom doorknob Anderson called from the den, "You ask why I don't live here, Honey, how come you don't move?" Though not original, it was her best line.

HE'S GONE

for Rebecca

The waiting. The goddamn hours stretching out like a winding sheet. She hated the waiting above all else. The apartment as still as a tomb. It was a tomb. Her thoughts were full of death, of endings. The apartment she loved for so long, her home, their home. They found it together. She found it. She called him and he came and he loved it straight away as she did.

"I knew you would love it," she told him.

"Yes," he said, "Yes, it's quite perfect for us, isn't it? There's a room there for my—for, you know—my—and another for you, next to the bedroom. It's a nice bedroom, isn't it?"

He loved it. He loved their apartment. So why did he stay away so much? Why had he been untrue to her? And, worse, why now, why is he gone forever? How could he do this to her? How could he leave her? Every day she had waited for him to come home. This is what the pregnancy brought them. Initially, she didn't want the baby, she made that clear. But he loved the idea of her pregnant.

"You'll have to quit your job, of course," he told her. "Won't that be delicious, just staying home, getting the room ready for the baby? Won't you love that?"

But she didn't love it. She waited every afternoon, every dead, long afternoon, for him to come home so she could tell him how awful it was, how the hours without him were torture for her. She told him she loved the baby, of course she did. What mother wouldn't? But she hated being alone. *Alone*—the word hurt.

But because of the baby she had all this time to herself. All those long days. The afternoons were the worst. As the light slipped from the sky, and she sat in her chair, a book propped open on her lap, a book she would never read, a dead book. The afternoons were deadly.

The apartment they had loved was a cage now. He must have thought so, he must have hated the apartment really to turn his back on it, on her. He had loved the apartment. It was their home. So now she hated the apartment. She hated its tasteful écru walls, its wood floors, its breakfast nook. She hated the bistro table, the bookcases, the brass sconces, the linen dromedary loveseat. She wanted out, out.

And now, just as she knew would happen, he had left her for good. He hated her whining. He hated her. He had never really loved her. Was it all pretend? Because she was pretty when she was young, pretty and easy going? She didn't know. She didn't know why he loved her. When he did.

Now that's all over.

She was abandoned. That's what they called it.

She sat in the chair and day would turn to dusk and dusk to midnight and she would be alone forever. When the baby came—when it did—and she had to decide—no. She would not think of that now. But, oh, how sorry he would be for leaving her—for leaving them. He would be so sorry.

She sat and waited. She sat in the chair that faced the door. The apartment ticked like a ship in harbor, beams settling, as if everything were in flux. But everything is not in flux. It's all settled. It's settled for all time. She knew what she would do—when it came—what she had to do. She was all alone. She had no one but him and he knew that and now he was gone. This time, this time he was gone for good.

She knew this day would come. She had told him so. You will leave me, she told him. I know it. Just when things get a little sticky, you will leave me. He had held her then, but there was reserve in his gestures. He was holding himself back. He was holding his loathing in check so that she would not know he was planning on leaving her.

And now it had come. That day had come. She was alone at last.

Now she looked at her book. Its pages made no sense to her. She didn't think she had really read that far in it. There was a bookmark. Had she put it there? The words in the book were inane. They mocked her.

She felt the baby move. It wasn't a kick, just movement, like something underwater that wants to see the light of day, something malevolent. She hated how it made her feel. She hated it when it moved.

Now she stared straight ahead. There were sounds in the hallway.

Probably that damned neighbor with her boyfriend, the fat musician who thought he could sing the old songs, the standards.

Now the movement stopped before her door. She straightened her spine.

A key turned in the lock. And the door opened and he came in.

He stopped before her. In his arms were flowers. He looked at her for a long time. His shoulders sagged. Wearily, he lay the flowers down on a table and knelt before her.

"What is it this time, dear?" he asked her. "Why are you crying today?"

"I thought you were gone for good," she said.

He sighed. It was an awful sound.

He put his head on her legs as if he had come from far away just to do that. They both were still for a while. She would not put her hands on his head. She would not.

"I thought you were really gone for good this time," she said.

Her words hung there in the air above them. He had no idea what to say next.

TRAVELER

I found myself in Y—, that strange country, with its treacherous terrain and tumultuous politics, its inedible foods and avid police squads. I was lost. I drove pointlessly, hopelessly, relentlessly. The mountains sprang up on all sides, closing in on me. The roads wandered, going in no noticeable direction. The car, a rental, seemed made of infirm materials and coughed and sputtered like an old man.

Suddenly, like a rift in dark clouds, a town appeared. It seemed to glitter in the murk. There were ramshackle houses, buildings colored dun and écru with brighter trim and small painted doors. There was an inn. My car shuddered under a small portico. I stopped and went inside. I was as tired as I had ever been, a great limb-heavy weariness that almost choked me.

The lobby resembled no lobby I had ever seen.

I stopped an old man in a military jacket.

"Is this the lobby?" I asked him. He obviously spoke no English and looked at me as if I had offered him drugs or my daughter.

Then I saw the desk, a desk that resembled a hotel's check-in. I approached warily. What if no one spoke English? Would I wander this strange town, voiceless and unanswered?

"Have you a room?" I asked the woman behind the counter. She was a heavy-set woman with a head like a dumpling. On her nose she sported a grisly wart.

"Yours is ready," she said.

I hesitated. "You have a room for me?" I asked for clarification.

"Oh, yes, all ready," she assured me.

She had me sign the register and handed me a key. It was made of a heavy metal, the kind of old-fashioned key you might see in horror movies. No one approached to pick up my bag so I hoisted it myself and went in search of the room. The woman smiled her encouragement as if I had solved a puzzle.

The corridors were dank and the walls seemed to sweat, a dark perspiration. I found the door which corresponded to the number carved into my key. I turned the key in the lock and it made a sound like a jailer's arrival.

I opened the door on a room nicer than I anticipated. It was an odd pink and orange room, pink dresser, orange walls, dirty orange carpeting. It was small but nicely appointed. I set my bag down by the dresser.

"Who are you?" a woman in the bed asked me.

I started, put my hand to my chest.

"This is my room," I said after a moment. She stared at me. She had the sheet pulled up to her chin. She was not unattractive, with that squarish face that many people in Y—had. "The woman downstairs assured me that this was my room."

"I don't know how to talk to you," the woman in the bed said.

I realized that she spoke English well. My heart began to calm.

"I can go downstairs and see if there is another room," I offered.

"There are no other rooms. They told me this," she said.

I stood there foolishly looking around at the walls.

"M-may I stay with you?" she asked me, finally.

I thought about this for a moment. What a strange impasse!

"First," I said. "Let me see your breasts."

She lowered the sheet. Her breasts were beautiful, as shapely as a new pair of shoes.

"Yes," I said. "I think it will be okay," I said.

She smiled now and I noticed that her teeth were bad. Her breasts were perfect but her teeth were terrible.

"Come into bed with me," she said. "You look tired."

"I am very tired," I said. And began to undress. When I was naked I stood beside the bed.

"Come on," she said, opening the sheet as if it were a tent flap.

"I am very tired," I repeated. "I thought I was lost."

I got in next to her. Her body was warm and smooth like fresh milk. She put her arms around me.

"But you are not lost," she said. "This is your room."

THE ONLY ONE-ARMED MAN
I EVER KNEW

The only one-armed man I ever knew was a housepainter named Les. This may sound like the beginning of a joke, but, don't laugh. The story of Les is a tragedy. Or so it seems to me.

I met Les when he joined our driveway basketball games. He was, I believe, a friend of Bobby's. Les was pleasant and affable and a surprisingly good shot. I was a bit cowed by Les—I didn't speak to him for a long time. I was afraid of the fierceness with which he played sports and I was afraid of his lost limb. I was the kind of youngster who was self-conscious around people who had disabilities, the disenfranchised of the world. It was almost Tourette's. I was afraid of saying something horribly inappropriate, something just plain horrible. This is, in itself, perhaps, horrible.

Later, Les became a friend. He and his wife came to dinner often. She was willowy, what we used to call a real dish. She had silky black hair which made her look slightly Asian. She also had a mouth like a drunken sailor. Her name was Ann.

Les and Ann looked good together. Les had a way of standing which made his impairment disappear, if you can picture an absence disappearing. Ann quickly became Shelley's best friend. Shelley was my wife.

Shelley and I married in a hurry, a bushwhack pregnancy, perhaps attained on our very first date. Shelley was 100 pounds of raw sexuality and self-centeredness. Shelley was dangerous and I knew it right away and it frightened me. When we married I put on a brave face. It was the face I was to wear for the next five years. The child we made died before we even named her. At the funeral Shelley turned to me and said, "Grace. I want to name her Grace."

Shelley and Ann made a formidable pair. They were so sexy that men were naturally attracted to them and approached them even if Les and I were present. This, for the most part, we took good-naturedly. Sometimes, if Les had had too much to drink, or if he had had a bad day, he exhibited a quick trigger and a furious and reckless physicality that frightened the suitors away. Only once in my presence did Les actually hit a man. It was in a dark bar. The man, a tall Swede, who had said something untoward to Ann, took one quick punch to the mouth and then, as he gathered his own fists, he realized Les only had one arm. You could see the air go out of him. He practically let Les beat his face red, only putting up token defensive arms, and apologizing even as Les's fists drove him backwards.

It didn't help when Les's business started failing. Independent contractors were still a pretty good commodity in our town and Les, given a more even temperament, would probably have continued to flourish. But, the drinking, the fights, and eventually the wife he couldn't keep at home, fashioned a tragic figure. Les began to diminish.

I could only stand on the sidelines and watch. I was no

help. Still, as an adult, I was that self-conscious youngster who was awkward with the world's uglier manifestations. I didn't know how to handle a friend who was both alcoholic and disabled. Truth be told, had Shelley and Ann not connected in the way they did, Les and I would not have stayed friends. And, when the women began to move away from us simultaneously, instead of being thrown together, Les and I drifted apart. There was no longer a point at which our lives touched, even tangentially.

When Shelley left me, and Ann Les, the world seemed a place of defeat and deprivation. A planet off-beam. I couldn't turn to the bottle like Les because I had a bad gut. So I took pills. Prescribed medicines for backache or pleurisy which I abused quickly, so quickly that I had to change doctors three times.

The last I heard from Les, he was in prison. Another fight, this time putting a guy in the hospital with a split pate. Les wrote me one short letter. It was pitiful. The scrawl of a child and the syntax of a slow sixth-grader. It made me tear up. He said he needed to talk or he was going to go crazy; he needed to feel connected somehow to his past.

I tried to find Bobby, someone who would help. I tried to pass the buck. I didn't deserve the onus that was Les. I didn't even like him that much. He wouldn't let me pity him, for he was stronger than I was. He had a fighter's strength; a battler, Les was. Which made his plea unseemly somehow. I never got in touch with Bobby and I never received another letter from Les. Eventually, I forgot about him and ceased to feel guilty about it. God knows where Ann is. I didn't even try to find her.

I heard from Shelley, once, also. She wrote from London where she was living with a potter. She wanted to know if I could find the antique brooch my mother had given her as a wedding gift. I had sold the thing the week Shelley left me. I never answered her either.

A WALK IN THE WOODS

—It's nippier than I thought.

—It's nice. These woods.

—Yes.

—Reminds me of other woods, other walks.

—Whose woods these are I think I know.

—When younger, when we were younger.

—I remember.

—That was quite a walk.

—And quite a long time ago.

—You were so

—impetuous.

—Youth.

—Not that you're less bold now.

—Well—

—I knelt in the grass before you. You leaned on a tree.

—I remember.

—A huge tree. A towering tree.

—Yes.

—A long time ago

.—Not so much.

—We were so young.

—How did we know? How—

—We didn't. We just went on. Life is

—just going on.

—We've been through a lot, done everything.

—It seems so at times, doesn't it?

—How free we were. How natural.

—Is this a trail? I wonder. Is this a path?

—I think so. Not—

—There. It goes around there.

—Yes.

—Beautiful, though, isn't it? The woods.

—Yes.

—Good to be outdoors, alone again.

—After all this time, alone again.

—The children.

—Well.

—We wanted that. We did. That was what we did.

—Yes. A family.

—Yes.

—Time passes. Impetuosity wanes.

—Yes.

—You were so beautiful. I remember, the first time I saw your breasts.

—Gone now. I hate that childbirth does that.

—No, now.

—It's true. How can you—

—You are beautiful still. I didn't mean that.

—I know.

—Then.

—Yes. Have we done it all, do you think? I want to do something else.

—What—

—Something we haven't done.

—It's the woods. You're remembering.

—Yes.

—That was lovely. You kneeling in the leaf-rot.

Corey Mesler

—It was. Your dick.

—Come now.

—Your lovely dick. In my mouth.

—Yes.

—We could do that again. I would kneel here.

—Woman. You.

—I will. Do you want to? Do you want to stop a while?

—I do want to stop. Here.

—Yes. Sit.

—A fallen tree. How long ago?

—Right.

—If only to rest. Can't quite hike like I used to.

—No.

—You look lovely. The sun is in your hair. Your cheeks are flushed. Madonna.

—Sweet man.

—I need to pee.

—It's anywhere you want. Only nature out here.

—Damn prostate.

—Is it bothering you again?

—Not really. Not much.

—Are you going back to Dr.—

172

—Yes. I mean, I know I must.

—Yes.

—It's just—

—I know. Me too. I think I'm due.

—That scare that time. You had better.

—I know.

—Are you cold?

—Not much.

—You want my jacket? I told you to put on—

—No. I mean, thank you, I'm fine. The sun here is—

—Like honey. Your face.

—Yes. Sitting here is nice.

—It is.

—I could stay here. I could sleep right here, under this tree. I could.

—The woodland creatures would weave garlands for your hair.

—Let's take off our clothes.

—Grimalkin.

—I mean it.

—We'd freeze.

—We wouldn't, you know. The sun is quite nice.

—We're too old to be nudists. Too old.

—Okay.

—I still have to pee.

—Stand up and pee.

—Yes.

—Sweet—

—Yes.

—Wait—

—Yes—

—Let me hold it.

—What.

—Your dick. While you pee.

—For Godsake.

—No, really. I've never.

—Just because.

—I know.

—Well.

—Come here. Stand this way.

—Now, Grimalkin.

—Just you. How do you do it?

—It's fairly easy

—just—

—Here. Take your trousers down more. There.

—Mm.

—Now. Do it. Pee while my hand is wrapped around it.

—Well—

—Just. Like this? Should I hold it like this?

—I'm not sure—

—What is it? Does this hurt?

—No, no. I'm not sure I can pee. With you.

—Really?

—Well, I'm not sure. I never could

—you know

—with someone else—

—Shy man.

—Yes.

—Here, how bout I just shake your balls a bit. That help?

—Not to pee

—perhaps—

—Okay. Let's just be calm. Think about peeing. Water. Think about water.

—Yes. Is this important to you?

—It is. Suddenly it is.

—Okay.

—There, there. Calm. I am just rolling it in my fingers. There, there

—Mm.

—Go ahead, Darling. Take your time.

—Mm, just—

—Yes—

—I do—

—I know.

—I will—

—I know. You have to pee. I feel it.

—I do

—I—

—Yes. There. Oh

—oh—there we go. Mm, it feels so warm. Mm, yes, I like the way it feels. Such a good stream, yes. Mm, that's my man—I like how warm it is. Your dick thick and warm.

—Oh—mm—you're getting your hand in it—

—Yes, I want to. I want to feel your pee, yes. Keep peeing. God, you were so full. It feels funny—your dick is so warm—and it feels—kind of throbby—I like it—I want my hands covered with your pee—there—God—

—Oh. My sweet. That was quite a pee.

—Yes. Yes, are you finished now?

—Yes. I am. I think.

—May I hold it just a while longer? While my hand is still warm with your pee?

—Yes. My knees are weak.

—There, there.

—You're a funny woman.

—There. Now. Zip up.

—Yes. Thank you.

—That was—magnificent! I won't wash this hand for a while.

—You're a funny woman. My Grimalkin.

—We'd never done that before.

—Okay.

—A memorable day. Don't you think?

—I do. Yes. Thank you.

—Thank you, darling. You pee very nicely.

—Thank you.

—Now, that path. Where does it go from here?

—I don't

—Is that it? Is that the path? Where do we go from here?

—I don't know. I don't have any idea.

THE VOICE AND ME

The Voice that Wants my Annihilation waits in line at the Jiffy Stop. I feign interest in the Hostess rack to avoid His eye. I hear Him ask, too loudly, for a lottery ticket. "Do not scratch here," the young Korean man says. The Voice looks around to see if anyone is witness. His gaze rakes over me like a small tool grooming its bonsai bed. It's too hot in the Jiffy Stop because outside it is too cold. After The Voice leaves I feel as if I should purchase something. I get some chemical cakes and the latest issue of *Boobs*. The young Korean man rings up my sale and smiles at me. "You writer," he says. I shake my head. What if The Voice that Wants my Annihilation were somehow still listening? I do not want Him to know of my ability to limn him in print, to mask my fear of him behind irony, lucubration, feminine rhyme or syzygy. As if He is an ex-wife, I want Him to think I still love Him. I go home and study the small pastry I have bought to see if there is something there about which to write a tanka. The phone rings. I know it is The Voice calling. I want so badly to finish something before I answer His call. I want so bad to finish one small thing before I answer His call.

THE REVIEWER, THE AUTHOR

Lemuel Pumpkin took his job seriously. Some said too seriously. But book reviewing is not for the faint of heart and if you can't take potshots at the great you should be working at Piggly Wiggly instead of passing judgment on the written word.

Reader: Lemuel Pumpkin's first byline had turned up in the Sunday book page suddenly, out of the roguish firmament, by way of Literary Kur, in solid block letters under a review of Joyce Carol Oate's latest novel. The headline said, "Oates Monthly Fiction Thin Oats." The byline said, "Lemuel Pumpkin is a local freelance writer."

Pause after preparatory comments. Commencement of actual story.

To begin: Lemuel wrote a review of a local writer's first novel, a writer who had spent many years laboring away at writing, having little success until he hit upon an interesting concept for a novel, wrote it in one year and had it published by the first small house he sent it to. Of course, Lemuel knew nothing of this. Nor should it color the way he did his job.

When *Mnemonics for the Devil* first fell into his lap he hated the title immediately. "Precious," he made a note on the book's last blank page before he ever started. By the time he had read the whole thing that back page was filled with multiplicitous adjectives, mostly pejorative. Jejune, immature, vegetative, risible, ruttish, churlish, agley, fatuous. The page swam with calumniate verbiage. *Mnemonics for the Devil* was raked across the coals.

Its author was a middle-aged man who wrote for the weekly liberal newspaper, *The Gleaner,* a column called "Cogitant and Incogitant." His name was Philip Roth, but he wrote under the name Lance Salina for obvious reasons.

When Lance picked up the Sunday paper and saw the cover of his humble little novel reproduced at the top of the reviews page his heart skipped school. He could almost not read the first line—he tried to read the whole review in one gulp, the way one swallows some foul-tasting medicament. He took a deep breath. The opening line cohered.

"If this first novel were a joke it would be a knock-knock joke."

Lance wasn't sure if this was good or bad.

"Such is its level of wit and sophistication."

Not good.

Lance Salina could barely take in the rest of the review. It was so, well, unkind. He couldn't find one positive word in the whole damn thing. His brow broke out in sweat, a sweat as thick as blood. He was Jesus in the Garden, right before, you know. He was lion feed. He was a poor gowk stuck on a planet where there was not one sympathetic soul.

Lance Salina's wife, a willowy—some would say skinny— brunette named Adrienne Salina, nee Hovind, found her husband sitting at his desk, the newspaper spilling from his lap. He looked like Marat in his tub.

"What?" she said, not unkindly.

"They hate it," Lance said.

"Phil," Adrienne said, taking her husband's flaggy hand. "They who? Hate what?"

"Everyone everywhere. They hate *Mnemonics for the Devil*."

His wife, who was having an affair with Lance's best friend, the editor of *The Gleaner*, quickly assessed the problem. The daily must have reviewed her husband's novel and reviewed it unkindly.

"Whatsit say?" she asked, petting her husband's hand, as if it were a kitten.

"Worthless. Shouldn't have been committed to paper. Author should give it up."

"Phil, it does not say that. Give it here."

Adrienne read the review as the silence of the lambs settled around them. Lance sat still in his chair, a tatterdemalion.

"Hm," she said. "Asshole."

"He's right," Lance said.

"He is not right," Adrienne said. "And after you've thought about it for a while you'll see that. How's *Fabricant* coming?"

Fabricant was Lance's second novel, still in the works, still a gummy hundred and fifty pages without shape or form.

"Never," Lance answered.

*

"He took it pretty hard," Adrienne said, lying next to Leonard Crisp, her lover.

"Well, it was pretty harsh. Who is this Lemuel Pumpkin? Surely, that's not his real name."

"I don't know," Adrienne said.

"We could find him and tie him to a pole and run him out of town. The old-fashioned answer."

"Ha," Adrienne said. "We could pull his pants down and throw him into the middle of Poplar Avenue."

"Now, you're thinking," Leonard said.

"It's got me kind of blue," Adrienne said. "Poor Phil."

"Yeah…" Leonard said. He pretty much had exhausted his sympathies and now wanted the willowy—some would say skinny—Adrienne to put her snow-soft mouth over his penis, which was engorged throughout this conversation.

"It's my job to bolster him," Adrienne said, looking into the middle distance as if it were a mirror.

Leonard pulled the covers back to reveal his need.

"Oh," Adrienne said. "Guess it's time to suck and fuck."

"Well put," Leonard said, even as he felt the sweet moistness slide over him like a mitten.

*

It was a few days later that Leonard Crisp while he was in line at the local health food store, slowly became aware of a heavy-set, perspiring man in front of him, buying what looked like every healthy snack food the store offered: Blue Corn Chips, White Cheddar Popcorn, No Oil Tortilla Chips, Baked Cheddar Puffs.

The man wore an oversize Hawaiian shirt, which even so, was stretched over his considerable belly. His hair hung in strands to his shoulders and appeared unwashed.

"Thank you, Mr. Pumpkin," the hippie cashier with the great breasts said.

"Mmf," Pumpkin replied.

Leonard Crisp did not understand the impulse which led him to drop his purchase and follow the stately, plump Mr. Pumpkin out the door. Surreptitiously, as if he were playing *Man from UNCLE*, Leonard crept to his car and just as surreptitiously crept into traffic behind the pea-green hatchback that the overweight reviewer bumped onto Madison Avenue.

Leonard Crisp followed him to a Midtown apartment building, pulled over to the curb and watched Lemuel Pumpkin park his car, get out and enter the building. He sat for a second in silent contemplation of what he had just done. He smiled.

Later, in bed again with the wife of his best friend, he offered up his information as if it were the Golden Fleece.

"I've found our Mr. Pumpkin," he announced, after they had begun preliminaries.

Adrienne stopped her ministrations.

"I didn't know we had a Mr. Pumpkin."

Now there was a war inside Leonard. He didn't want Adrienne to stop her exploration of his scrotal sac but he wanted to get her congratulations on a job well-done.

"I found out where this Pumpkin character lives. I followed him home. It's not far from here. It's in Midtown." He was stumbling for coherence.

"And this does what for us?" Adrienne rightly asked.

"Well," Leonard began. Suddenly he didn't know.

"I suppose I should tell Phil ..."

This was better.

"Yes," Leonard said, cautiously.

"Maybe I better call him. It might cheer him up to know you cared enough to ferret out his nemesis."

"Well," Leonard said, and he put his palm over his lover's moist and furry crotch.

"Mm," Adrienne couldn't help saying. "After, I guess."

"Yes," Leonard said. "After I lick you into a tumult."

"Okay," Adrienne allowed, settling back on the pillow, her arms smugly behind her head.

*

"Leonard found out where this Pumpkin character lives," Adrienne told her husband, as blithely as possible, over buttering the toast one morning.

Lance looked blankly at his wife. He saw through her as if she were made of plexiglass. He could see the bird feeder in the backyard, where a brouhaha was heating up over the newly filled feeder.

"When did you see Leonard?" he said, finally.

"Ran into him at Square Foods," Adrienne said, perhaps too quickly.

"Mm," Lance said. Now he was studying his toast.

"He thinks we should do something."

"Something," Lance said, looking up.

"Yes. We shouldn't let this pusillanimous nobody punish your first novel without remorse. He should suffer some recrimination."

"Maybe just a letter," Lance said. "We could get Bobby to write it."

Bobby was the high-school kid who cut their lawn.

"Bobby?" Adrienne said with more heat than she intended. "Jesus, Lance. Let's think big here."

"Why?" Lance said.

Adrienne let out a long breath.

"How's *Fabricant?*" she said, switching gears.

"Stillborn," Lance said. And with that he got up from the table and went into his study to stare at the computer screen and maybe play a few rounds of solitaire.

Adrienne found her husband infuriating. It was enough to drive her into her lover's arms. She picked up the phone to call Leonard.

*

But Adrienne never called Leonard. When she began to dial she realized there was someone on the line.

"Hello?" Adrienne said, after a few numbers.

"Hello?" came the answer.

"Hello?"

"Hello?"

"Hello?" Adrienne tried again. "Who's there?"

"Is Lance Salina there?" the voice said.

"Yes," Adrienne said.

There was an undersea silence.

"May I speak with him?"

"Yes," Adrienne said. Still she held the receiver.

More time passed. Somewhere another novel was published.

"Who may I say is calling?" Adrienne fluttered.

"Pumpkin," the voice said. "Lemuel Pumpkin."

*

The phone call seemed to take forever. Adrienne sat in the kitchen playing with her coffee, stirring it, sipping some from her spoon, dripping some onto the tabletop to paint with. She was as nervous as a watch.

She finally had to ease the receiver off its cradle and listen. The line was still open but there was a strange silence there, something like the silence right before the mob explains something to a stoolie.

At 10:38 a.m. Lance emerged from his study. He was still wearing pajamas and a housecoat, the sash of which dragged behind him like a dead tail.

He walked by his astonished wife and fixed himself another cup of coffee.

"Jesus, Phil!" Adrienne exploded.

Lance jumped.

"What did he want?"

"Who?" Lance asked, feckless, unfettered.

"Fucking Pumpkin ... on the phone ... the fucking reviewer," Lance's willowy wife sputtered.

"Oh. To talk."

"About what? Did you read him the riot act about that pissy review?"

"No, no. No need for that."

Lance seemed to be talking from a great distance. He seemed to be someplace else.

"Did you even discuss the review?"

"Oh, yes, sure. He said he'd been up all night."

"As if that forgives it."

"Hm?" Lance said.

Adrienne looked into her husband's whiskered, uncaring face. She loved him, still. But she thought he'd been bodysnatched. She grabbed her car keys and stormed out the door, an ill wind.

*

Adrienne pushed Leonard backwards into the room, without greeting. She began taking her clothes off, silent as the eyeless statues of Greece.

Leonard watched. He enjoyed watching the thin body of his lover emerge from its clothing. He enjoyed this pro-active Adrienne, this hothead.

He sat back on the bed, fully clothed, still even in his trenchcoat. Adrienne stood in the middle of the room, skin pimpled with chill, small-breasted, with small wings for hips and a snatch of tangled static over her crotch that was as complex as The Iliad.

Suddenly, her anger sank within her like a dying star and she stood naked and embarrassed. Her lover smiled. Not knowing what else to do she knelt before him and undid his belt, taking his member out into the air, pulling on it as if it were a slot machine.

"Ah," Leonard said.

Some of Adrienne's power returned. She brought her husband's best friend off in her mouth, swallowing with aplomb. She gave his sinking ship a slap before sending it back to its dock.

"Ow," Leonard said, zipping up. "Okay. Who are you mad at?"

"Apparently Phil and Lance, I mean, Phil and this Pumpkin character are friends."

Now Leonard sat up straight.

"Tell me everything," he said. The game was afoot.

*

Here's the truth. You shall know this before our secondary characters, whom we will leave spent and flummoxed because they deserve it for their duplicity.

Phil/Lance was actually Phil/Lance/Lemuel. Lance Salina, or Phil Roth, had split. Even he doesn't know why, but he found himself one dim afternoon, six months earlier, sitting at his keyboard, metaphorically, or literally if you wish, pulling at his hair, unable to think of a single word. He wasn't blocked. He was dying.

Suddenly there was another man sitting in the room with him. He looked sad, a street-person, disheveled, unkempt, distressing.

"What the hell?" Lance said, jumping backwards.

"Lance?" the man spoke tentatively.

"How the—who are—what?"

"I'm sorry," the ghostly figure said. Lance was worried about the new carpeting in his study, this guy was so sullied.

"Sorry?"

"For just breaking off like this. I didn't know what else to do. You were, well, it was inevitable. There was a crack, you see ..."

"Make sense, man. I'm this close to calling the police."

"I'm you," the man said, falling back in his seat as if exhausted. As if he had finally cleared things up.

"You're me?" Lance said. He put his hand on the telephone.

"I had to break off. You can see that."

"No, I ..."

"You were torn."

"Well, metaphorically ..."

"There is no metaphorically in my realm. In our realm," the stranger who was not a stranger answered.

It took several discussions to convince Phil/Lance of the reality of his second self. It took a lot of back and forth, to and fro, up and down.

After hours of conversation there was a lull. Lance had settled back in his chair and seemed to accept whatever was happening, whatever would happen next.

Finally, the disheveled eidolon spoke again.

"I need a name," he said.

And so it was that Philip Roth/Lance Salina named his other self. He chose the name because of his fondness for Nathanael West's work, and, even though he misremembered the character's name slightly, it stuck. It stuck like a drawer. It stuck like cobbler's wax.

Lemuel Pumpkin was born.

*

Meanwhile, back at the love den, the adulterers were scratching their heads, that is, their own heads, not each other's. They are not monkeys.

"But if he knows him, why is he so upset with the review? Why is he upset to the point of giving up the writing game?" Leonard asked the naked, supine Adrienne.

"Hell if I know," she answered.

"Maybe because they are friends. Maybe betrayal is at the heart of this, not just simple bad reviewing."

"But why the secrecy?" Adrienne asked.

Leonard rested his hand on his lover's rump. He petted it as if it were a live mink.

"Why the secrecy?" he repeated.

"Could it be——" suddenly Adrienne sat up. Leonard moved his hand to her soft, flat midsection. "Could it be that they are, um, you know, involved?'

"Lovers?"

"Right."

"Why would you jump to that conclusion? Phil not fulfilling his husbandly duties."

"Well, of course not. Why else would I be here?"

"Thank you, my dear," Leonard said, removing his hand.

"Oh, hell, Leonard, you know, you know how I feel."

Truth was that she felt nothing. She just needed Leonard for his priapus. She needed laying, and not just occasionally. It's a time-honored raison d'être.

Now she began shuffling into her clothes.

"Going?" Leonard asked, little-boy hurt in his voice.

"I've got to see to Phil. I've got to stay close to home for a while, see how this thing plays out."

"What is this thing?"

"Well, that's the question, isn't it?" Adrienne said, bending to buss the top of Leonard's head, a Judas kiss.

*

That evening, Adrienne scooted up next to her husband on the couch, where he was immersing himself in the who-cares-who-done-it of a paperback mystery. She tucked her bare feet up under her, like a school girl. She was feeling loopy, mystified and, oddly enough, shy.

"Dear," Adrienne said. This should have been enough to snap our hero to attention, "dear" being a moniker his wife did not toss his way very often.

"Hm?" he answered from within the confines of a pie plant in 1930s London.

"Look at me," Adrienne said. She was uncomfortable with her new feeling of incomprehension toward her husband. She was used to thinking of him as a finished puzzle.

Phil looked at his wife. Her hair was falling over one eye, her lips were wet. She looked seventeen.

"Tell me about this Pumpkin character."

"Tell you about him," Phil parroted.

"Yes, well, you know, how you know him. Where did ya'll meet and when? You seemed so upset by his review. And, if you're friends..."

"We're not friends," Phil/Lance said quickly.

"So, then..."

"The review stung. We are acquaintances. We have some things, some people, um, particulars in common. I naturally assumed he, if he reviewed *Mnemonics*, would be benevolent toward me, my first novel, local writer, you know, you expect..."

"Yes, of course. But, how do you know this man? He's a stranger to me and I thought ..."

"You may have run into him," Phil said, impassively.

"Really? I don't remember."

"He's not very memorable. An execrable character, really. A cipher. He's barely there, half a man."

Adrienne laughed a short bark.

"Well, what's he doing reviewing at the paper?"

"I don't know. I don't know how that got started."

"But you've, what, spent time with him?"

"Yes."

"When?"

"Adrienne, why all the questions? It's a non-issue. Let's drop it."

"You're so mysterious," Adrienne said to her previously unremarkable husband, and as her mouth formed the word "mysterious" he became that to her. She did not know beforehand that this subtle shift was taking place.

"Mm," Phil/Lance said and began to return to London.

Suddenly, Adrienne's hand was on her husband's thigh and since he was wearing loose, khaki shorts, it was skin to skin, and sent goose pimples honking up his leg and into his crotch.

He looked at his wife again. Twice in one night he looked at her.

Now her hand was slightly inside his shorts, her fingertips playfully under the material. And she was looking deeply into his eyes, licking her lips.

"Adrienne," Phil whispered. He had nothing to say.

The tips of her nails now touched his scrotum and were moving subtly up and down, lightly shaking his loose sack. His erection was as obvious as the gloss on a new hat.

And when she closed her hand around it was sudden and it was as if something new between them was busy being born. It had been a long time. And when she blew him and didn't even expect a returned favor, Phil was set to wondering. He came in her mouth. She lifted her head slowly. She, one final time, licked her lips, this time for maintenance's sake. And she smiled at her husband. It was an evening of many things formerly dead, revived.

*

So began the recrudescence of the marriage of Philip Roth and Adrienne Roth née Hovind. A period of great efflorescence and re-joining. And though Phil did not understand what precipitated such a rediscovering of their initial courting spark, he intuited that it had something to do with his alter ego. Or he feared this.

And what of Leonard, the ersatz adulterer, editor, best friend? He was left out in the cold. He started screwing young women and using pay-by-the-hour motels. He began an affair with a seventeen-year-old intern at the paper who thought Leonard was her key to the cultural elite of the city, if the city could be said to have a cultural elite. We leave Leonard now for a while. We leave him to stew in his own juices.

All went well for Phil/Lance now that his marriage found its feet again. He began, in earnest, to start to shape and re-design *Fabricant*. He fell in love with the title again. It spoke to him about his own life, about where he was going, about his emergent potential. *Fabricant*. And he stopped showing up for work at *The Gleaner*. Leonard could say little. Out of guilt he kept Lance on the payroll.

*

Meanwhile, in his Midtown apartment, crowded with a bed, a desk, a computer and little else, Lemuel Pumpkin kept busy pounding out reviews, as if he were the final word. Often he felt that way. That books came to him for their final assignment: either he would send them to perdition or he would boost their author upward on the ladder to Oprahdom. This was ridiculous, of course, in the backwater town where Lemuel did his work, but leave him his illusions, even if he is a simulacrum. Even simulacra need hope.

But increasingly, he felt the words coagulate in his head. He couldn't say what he meant to say about anything. He felt like a high-schooler beginning his book report, "I really liked this book."

Soon he was to put into motion the events that would bring this whole affair to its zenith. But patience, reader. A few more preliminary scenes, some domestic bliss, some minor antagonism, some sex, a little more character development. All will happen in its own time. All will appear to happen as if inevitable.

*

"Your friend Pumpkin has a review in the paper today," Adrienne said, dipping her folded toast into her coffee.

Phil/Lance was engrossed in the box scores from the NBA.

"Mm?" he answered.

"Pumpkin," Adrienne repeated.

"Yes, sweet?"

"No. Pumpkin. Lemuel. He's got a review in the paper." Phil looked up.

"Of course he does, dear. He's a book reviewer. Who is he trashing this week?"

"Well, it appears to be a rave."

"Good for Lemuel. He can do something other than attempt to ruin writer's careers."

"He writes, 'The author might be the American Flaubert, an artist whose every word resonates craftsmanship—intelligence and imagination in equal parts'."

"Whoa. Those are strong words. I'm sure Lemuel means them, as much as he means anything."

Lately, Lance has seemed unassailable, immune to the scarification left by Pumpkin's review of *Mnemonics for the Devil*, immune, really, to ill words from any quarter. He was deep into *Fabricant* and happiest when working on its thorny narrative complexities.

"Who is he calling the American Flaubert?" Lance asked casually.

Adrienne hesitated a beat.

"Liz Grandmonde."

Lance almost lost the swallow of coffee in his throat. After mastering the muscle control required getting it to go down he sat stock still. His glazed look was the same nosferatu stare from the morning of the *Mnemonics* review.

"Phil?" Adrienne said, gently.

"Sh-she's a hack," he said with a rasp.

"She's your friend, Phil. You should be happy for her."

"Happy for her? Happy for her? He's doing this to get at me. Don't you see? He doesn't think her backwash is literature—he's trying to get my goat by overpraising the only other local writer who writes serious novels, if you can call her imitation Ellen Gilchrist serious."

Phil was sputtering.

"Well ..." Adrienne began.

"I can't let this just pass."

"I don't see that..."

"I'll write a letter. I'll ..."

"Phil, let me ..."

"I'll go see the editor there. I'll wring his cowardly chicken neck."

"Well, that's ..."

"I'll hunt Pumpkin down like a dog. I'll carve him like a jack-o'-lantern."

"Phil ..."

"I'll have to kill him. Of course. That's the solution."

"I hardly think ..."

"I'll poison him. I brought him into the world. I can exeunt him from it."

"What are you ..."

"Adrienne, say something. I'm boiling over here."

"Dear," Adrienne said. Her fluffy, white robe, loosely sashed, fell open and her warm, willowy nakedness shone beneath like ambergris.

"I'm going out," Phil stood, upsetting the coffee carafe. "I'm going to go buy some poison."

Adrienne could only stare as her husband went out the door. She didn't really care if he had just become a murderer. She was more concerned that the sight of her glimmering belly and her curly Y failed to arouse her husband. Lately the sex had been so good.

*

Let's return briefly to our semi-antagonist, Leonard Crisp. Today we find him at the Palomino on Summer Avenue, in a rent-a-room, with young Albertine Ross, the 17-year-old intern. Albertine lay face down on the acrylic bedspread, clad only in a thong—her signature piece of clothing, and how Leonard will remember her for the rest of his life. Leonard sat on the edge of the bed, smoking a cigarette. The scene looked post-coital but, as of yet, the pair have only undressed.

Albertine was busy looking at an *In Style* magazine. Leonard was thinking about Adrienne, and hence Lance. He had read the Grandmonde review, also. And it gave him pause. More than ever he wanted to confront this Pumpkin character, this street-Arab book reviewer, this miscreant.

And he knew where he lived.

"Nice tits," Albertine said.

"Eh?" Leonard half turned.

Albertine held up an ad for something-or-other. The impossibly arcuate model was dressed as was Albertine and was staring at the camera with a fuck-you expression on her lippy face. Her breasts were indeed spot-on.

And now Leonard's attention was drawn to the fresh backside before him, its callipygian deliciousness a pure sensory implosion. He had a brief thought that he would stub his cigarette out on one of Albertine's orbicular halves. Instead he used the ashtray next to the bed.

Readers, you have been promised at least one more sex scene and you, who have stood by, so soldierly , shall have it.

Leonard leant over now, and instead of a glowing cigarette end, he placed his tongue on Albertine's left buttock. He licked it as one would lick an all-day sucker. He employed one of his hands to knead the other side, thus attacking the aforementioned hill from both sides. So far his ministrations were having no effect: he heard a page turn.

He moved his tongue to the string-covered crack and ran his tongue down its length. As he reached the fundament he was relieved to hear a sigh escape from above. He spent some time there with his lubricious engagement. It was easy to slide further down to the teen's sweet sex and, as Albertine raised her rear like a rutting mammal, Leonard pulled aside the thin material of her thong and began cunnilingus in earnest.

"Oh, Jaysus," Albertine said.

She flipped over, simultaneously slipping out of the only piece of clothing she had on. A move perhaps only to be attempted when young.

As Leonard tunneled, Albertine was pulling at his waist, moving him ass over her steaming teakettle.

Soon they were the sign of Cancer, crabbed onto that tiny bed, Leonard's legs bent awkwardly on the fake wood headboard. Albertine ground her hand against the front of Leonard's briefs, underneath which he was as hard as the push of death.

"Aggh," Leonard said.

And, in response, his lovely lover pulled him out into the room, where he stood up straight, the class's prize pupil, eager to be taught, practically saying, "Go on, go on."

Albertine took Leonard into her young mouth and with the relish only the young put into such ministrations sucked and sucked, while she herself was enjoying the learned tongue and lips of the older and wiser Leonard Crisp.

And, readers, if you must suspend disbelief here, do it for the sake of the story which really must get going again. We have to move on. My fellow voyeurs and revelers, take one last look at our naked duo.

Just so: Our lovers came together. A simple enough statement. They *came* together. Slightly more precise. But, in particular, in this context, here, it means: as Albertine felt the growing pressure at the top of her pubis, as the flow of sensation began to spread through her entire crotchal area, Leonard flew into her mouth, a flood of warmth, a bodily humor; not funny, really, almost loving, a release as of a homing pigeon who will never return.

And, afterwards, as both lovers lay next to each other, simultaneously wiping mouths, Leonard Crisp spoke the most unromantic thing he'd ever said after sex:

"Adrienne thinks Lance knows this Pumpkin."

*

So Leonard Crisp lost his teenage lover. No surprise there; the attention span of the young wanders lonely as cloud, strays like a gliding ghost, up and down the world, a noble Morninger. He wept and moved forward. Or he wept and remained still, stalled, stuck.

He called Adrienne late at night and cooed, and she hung up as if the sound of his once-seductive voice was an auctioneer's.

Where are we?

Leonard: alone.

Adrienne: living on the edge, newly, again, in love with her husband, intrigued by what she perceives as his enigmatic worldliness.

Phil/Lance: immersed in *Fabricant*, a tale told by a sage, whistling through the canyons of the modern city like a vulture's cry, wise as a woodcock.

Lemuel: writing reviews frantically, a book a week, a book every three days, sweat gathering on his prodigious brow like swarming fire-ants, writing as if his days were numbered, like this: 100, 99, 98, etc. Writing nonsense, unpublishable nonsense.

Albertine: sweet Albertine, a mere sidebar to this story, now busy sucking off Jimmy Rowinger, the high-school quarterback, who, it may be imagined, comes too early, too often, too solipsistically.

Jimmy: (sere, transitory leaf caught in the story's updraft) living la dolce vita.

Bobby: (the kid who cuts lawns) just lost his virginity to Beth Denmark, white-haired cheerleader, thin as an anchorite. Happier than a pig on a church organ.

Beth: (see Bobby).

The hippie cashier with the great breasts: days she sells tofu and tamari, nights she does drugs and strips at Platinum Plus.

Okay.

*

Now, as we strive toward dénouement, the shore is in sight, the sailors are dying of thirst, things get thornier, people become more difficult to manipulate, stubborn and insubordinate, recalcitrant relationships try to cloak themselves in cloud just as we try to reveal them, dissect them, clarify things. It's a cat's cradle is what it is.

Everyone wants a dovetail. It is built into human DNA to hope for full realization.

We shall see.

The sad impasse Leonard Crisp discovered in his middlescence brought him to the Roths' doorstep one drizzly Saturday morning, his hair plastered to his forehead like a helmet. His white shirt looked diaphanous from the moisture. In short, he looked, and felt, a fool.

"Leonard," Adrienne said as she opened the door, her face squinching up as if it were made of rubber.

"I'm, well, I'm sorry, Ade," Leonard said.

"Look," Adrienne said, though she had no follow-up.

"Who is it?" Phil called from the kitchen, where he was once again lost in the pattern of perambulating birds in his backyard. So many of them walking around as if they had forgotten how to fly.

"And don't call me Ade," Adrienne said, as if she were finishing a thought.

"Can I come in? I'm getting soaked here," Leonard said.

Adrienne stepped aside, not so much an invitation as a matador's maneuver, postponing the kill.

Leonard slipped in, hopped through the living room and into the kitchen, where Phil sat in his pajamas, lost in the outside world.

"Phil," Leonard said, shaking like a golden retriever.

"Lance," Leonard said just as his addressee was turning to see what this commotion was that was disturbing his Saturday morning.

"Leonard," he said, inflection gone, his voice on flatline.

"I love your wife," Leonard said and tried to stand upright, tried to forget how he might look, a myrmidon, a doused Jack tar.

"Indeed," Phil/Lance said. And he was truly fascinated.

"I've been having intercourse with her for some time now and…"

It was just then that Adrienne stepped into the kitchen and struck Leonard across the back of his head with a plaster-of-paris bust of Goethe someone had given Lance years ago when one of his short stories won a regional award. The bust was just heavy enough to coldcock the unfortunate Leonard, who fell like a sack of kittens onto the kitchen linoleum. He lay there, silenced, a sodden tar baby.

"Jesus, Adrienne. Did you kill him?" Phil asked.

"I can only hope so," Adrienne said, but the tremor in her voice betrayed her fear.

"He's certainly very still," Phil said, still not rising from his chair, staring at the prostrate adulterer as if he were a simple stain.

Adrienne nudged him with the toe of her bare foot.

"Ung," Leonard said.

"The bastard's not dead," she said.

"Okay," Phil said. "So, he says you've been fucking."

"He didn't say fucking."

"A fine distinction."

"Well, it was true. We were. But it was because we weren't. I mean, you and I."

"Uh huh."

"I needed it. You were so, what were you?, so not there."

"Uh huh."

"Stop saying uh huh and get mad, damn you. I cheated on you. With your best friend. But, Phil, dear, it's over, it's been over. Ever since we, you know…"

"We started doing it again."

"Well, yes."

"Like crazed squirrels."

Adrienne almost laughed. It was what they used to say when they were young and courting. She almost laughed but she was still unsure of her husband's attitude toward this.

"Honey, I just want him out of here. For good. I want him out of our lives. It's good that this happened. It brings things to a head, it finishes it, do you see? Just a little?"

"Uh huh."

Adrienne nudged the body again, not for response this time but for something to do while she waited.

"I've never fucked anyone else," Phil said. He appeared to be thinking this over. "Never. You've been my only lover. I suppose this puts me in some sub-sub-category by myself, some freak of modernity. I'm practically a virgin."

"Oh, sweet," Adrienne said and rushed to her husband's side. She stood beside him holding his head and stroking it.

"I suppose I should," Phil said, after a moment.

"Should?" Adrienne said. She felt a lump in her stomach turn over.

"Fuck somebody else, I mean. I mean, it's only fair now. It's like you've given me a ticket."

Adrienne kept stroking her husband's head. They stayed like this for an inordinate amount of time. Meanwhile Leonard began to stir.

"The door is open," came a husky voice from the living room.

And just as Leonard sat up, in walked Lemuel Pumpkin, in a second-hand trench coat, looking like a wild-eyed madman, a street-person with troubles.

"The door is open," he repeated.

"What the hell do you want?" Lance said, sitting up straighter.

"We got business," Pumpkin said, all swagger now, sensing the situation was strange and hence ripe for exploitation.

"I've got no business with you," Lance said and he stood.

Simultaneously, Leonard Crisp stood. He wobbled. He put a hand to the back of his head.

"Holy Christ," he said. "Who hit me?"

"I did, you asshole," Adrienne said.

"What with, a fireplace poker? You could have killed me."

"I hit you with Goethe."

"Hey," Lemuel Pumpkin said, feeling the conversations were slipping away.

"What exactly do you want, Pumpkin?" Lance said.

"Get the hell out of our house," Adrienne said, but it was unclear whom she was addressing.

"I'm blocked," Pumpkin said.

Lance looked at him for a long time. Something was becoming clearer. Leonard Crisp slumped against the refrigerator. He looked like he was about to cry.

"Blocked, eh?"

"And you know why, you unforgiving demiurge."

"What?" Adrienne said. She looked about the room for a compatriot. She was unsure where she was.

"Give me some coffee," Pumpkin said. He felt like a gangster in charge of a roomful of gulls.

It was a spur-of-the-moment fix, really, though Lance had mentioned poison before. It was so handy, now, when the moment came. It bloomed like a tourbillion in front of him now. His course was set. The rat poison was beneath the kitchen sink. The Mr. Coffee just above it.

Still, he hesitated.

He hesitated because he wanted to make something clear before the end.

"You're blocked," he said, moving to the sink and getting a coffee mug from the cabinet as he talked.

"I, I can't write a damned word. And you know why."

"I think I do."

"You're writing again, you bastard. You're sucking me dry."

"Hm," Lance said, opening the door beneath the sink.

"It's my livelihood. It's all I've got," Pumpkin said. He sounded more like a small child than the one in control.

Lance sifted the rat poison into the coffee as one would a tablespoonful of Cremora. He added Cremora next.

"When I write, when my creative juices flow, yours cannot."

"Bastard," Pumpkin repeated, taking the proffered cup.

"Well, I made you and, it appears, I can unmake you."

"I'll see you in hell first," Lemuel Pumpkin said, taking a big swallow of coffee.

"What the hell are y'all talking about?" Leonard Crisp said.

Adrienne was studying her husband. She had a notion, an absurd notion, but one close to the truth. She saw the relationship between Lance and Lemuel whole, she saw it for what it was. A nightmare. A deadly dream.

And she saw her husband put the Talon G into Lemuel Pumpkin's coffee.

"Shut up," Pumpkin said to Leonard Crisp.

"Okay," Leonard said. His headache became acute. He thought perhaps he was going blind.

"You're gonna quit writing, see?" Pumpkin said.

"You sound like some cheap B-movie knock-off mug. You're even losing your ability to make mellifluous sentences."

"Fuck you," Pumpkin said. "And your coffee sucks, too," he added.

He reached up toward his head. He and Leonard looked like Castor and Pollux, both holding their addled heads. But only one of them was dying.

"Fuck you," Pumpkin whispered. It was the last thing he ever said.

*

Leonard Crisp helped the Roths bury the unnaturally heavy, corpulent corpse of the simulacrum book reviewer. They buried him underneath the bird feeder where he would for all eternity be the beneficiary of bird droppings and cracked seeds, the effluvium left over from the voracious appetites of our avian friends.

Afterward, wet from the diminishing drizzle and from sweat, the three sat at the Roths' kitchen table, a silence spread over them like a tarp. Phil/Lance put on a fresh pot of coffee.

After a long stillness, Leonard looked at the faces of his two friends. They seemed beatific. He thought, they just might be saints, paracletes.

"Rat poison?" he said.

Phil nodded.

"Fitting," Leonard said.

The tarp descended again.

The sun struggled out from behind the torn sheets of cloud. The backyard seemed lit by fairy lights.

"You and I are finished, you know?" Adrienne said to Leonard, her husband as witness.

Leonard looked at her. She was beautiful, like a painting of the Madonna. He thought about her willowy—some would say skinny—white, naked brilliance.

"Yes," he said.

Phil turned to the window again, his window, his view of the multivariate world.

The birds were flocking around the feeder as if they had discovered paradise, as if the feeder were the only place they had ever found sustenance. They were cacophony and camarilla.

"Look at those damn birds," Phil said, as if to himself.

Adrienne looked, too.

Leonard Crisp looked.

Then Leonard stood and left. His tale was told. He was gone gone.

Adrienne slipped her hand under her husband's arm.

"I love you," she said.

Phil/Lance looked at her. Her eyes were the glass walls that fence the secret darkness of unknown time.

"And I you," he said, somewhat stiffly and formally.

"You're not really going to fuck anyone else, are you, my sweet?" Adrienne said, putting her hand back into her husband's hair.

Lance just turned away, turned toward the world, where anything is feasible, where stories get made up and either come alive or don't. A world where love is still possible, and sex, vitalizing sex, just a wish away.

THE WORLD WENT AWAY

"How nice objects are—I'm glad we live in a thingy world."
—Iris Murdoch

The morning was as cold as clapboards. Jake stood next to his bed, a lifeless automaton. Jake needed the command to move. Only Jake had it.

He shook like a wet dog and put one foot in front of the other. The bed was a liferaft, around which he had to swim. To set out on open waters. The bed neither spoke nor shimmied.

Jake found his way into the bathroom, white as charnel bone. In the mirror was Jake's face looking at him, assessing. His eyes were glowing filaments. He knew the face and the face knew him. He abrogated the night's congeries.

In the kitchen the light seemed muted, like a Miles solo. Perhaps it was only Jake's smudged visualization. Progressing like a sleepwalker, Jake made a cup of coffee and while he waited for the appliance to percolate, he scavenged for bread. The wheat was moldy. The white hard. The rye held out the best possibility; it was apparently indestructible, the hardy rye.

Jake settled down with his breakfast and life slowly leached into him. He could feel his limbs loosening, his body returning, his heart engaging. And it was about this time that Jake began to sense something odd, something off-kilter.

The light. Something was wrong with the light.

He turned, stood, gazed out his kitchen window.

He had gone blind.

No, it wasn't blindness. Everything beyond his own kitchen window was gone. The world was white space, blank as a skull, as empty of *matter* as windswept dunes. Emptier. The dunes themselves were gone.

Was this the morning of dispossession?

Was Jake dead? Jake asked.

Jake turned toward the center of his home. He tottered to the front door—his mind was blank also, something tunneling there, slowly—and opened it as if he were opening his own tomb. Outside was the same emptiness, the same world gone white. Seemingly, only Jake and his house existed. Beyond his stoop. a void.

Jake stared into the nothingness for as long as he could. Madness lay that way.

His mind switched to reference mode: what had Kierkegaard said about the void?

Finally he turned back toward his home and relished its solidarity, its things. There was his couch, dusty and wavery like a couch underwater. There was his coffee table, his bowl of seashells, his *Newsweek* magazine. There his TV, his DVD player, his complete *Secret Agent Man* DVD set, his lamp—the one his ex-wife gave him after the divorce. A peace offering. A peaceful lamp.

His rooms were as stable as red bricks. And he was real; that was important. His brain worked, firing—in his thoughts a universe. A reconstructed, reconfigured world. It could be.

Jake sat down in a shabby rocking chair, covered with an old afghan. His hand felt the material underneath it; absentmindedly Jake was connecting himself to what was left. What was left?

Surely this was a temporary aberration. A glitch in space-time. Jake believed such things possible, and in his belief, he was comforted. It did not seem a time to panic.

So the outside world was gone. As gone as the Mayans. As gone as last night's dream. Funny; Jake did not think that he was *now* in a dream—this was not dreamspace, cloudland. This was the Earth, the old familiar Earth, though disappeared.

The TV suggested itself to Jake. The lifeline. Jake picked up the controller and pushed power. There was a satisfying click as the engines engaged, as the motor of the outside world began to whirl inside this box of glass and plastic.

And the show that Jake found on every channel was this: Nothing. Brought to you by the Imps of the Perverse. Sponsored by The Old Gooseberry Himself.

Every channel a white screen, a palette, a sheet upon which the soul of Man longed to record its heroic journey.

Jake laughed a sardonic laugh. Okay, everything was gone. Everything. Everydamnthing. He was Robinson Crusoe, and like Crusoe, he had been set adrift from the ordinary. This was, perchance. a plus.

Another possible plus: along with the rest of the known universe, his place of business was no more. No work for Jake, not on this day.

But, *had* the whole universe disappeared? Jake only knew that outside his residence, his own dwelling, there was a pane of white like sightlessness. What if one pushed *through* it? Perhaps the nothingness only extended for a hundred yards, or a mile. Jake could go out and explore it—he could find his way back. That was what people did—they explored the unknown—this was humanness. Jake felt grounded and, to be honest, a bit disappointed. If this were just a subtracting of his immediate surroundings it was an anomaly, sure, one that Jake could dine out on, as they say, but it was not the total obliteration his heart now secretly yearned for. He was possibly not the last man on Earth.

For argument's sake, let's say Jake is alone. Completely alone as no man has been since pre-Eve. What to do? How to feed; what if he got sick? how would he pass the many minutes in each day?

Jake stayed in his chair, contemplating this.

An hour or so passed.

Finally, Jake admitted that he had to go outside. He had to chance it. Because what if later the world returned, and he had to explain what he had done, and he had done nothing? Jake was even now mulling over what other people would think. Is this basic humanness, too? This insecurity?

Jake dressed as if going on a hike. Shorts, socks, boots. Into the many pockets of his shorts he squirreled away the items of survival. GORP, lighter, knife, paper, pen. And he hooked a bottle of water to his belt. Intrepid voyager.

Jake once more stood in his doorway, his threshold the last solid thing for miles, perhaps for miles. Jake now half-expected the world to click back in, to reload like a recalcitrant webpage. But he only saw white ahead, only zilch. Jake had no pathway. Jake had no direction. What if he got out into it, whatever it was, and could not tell up from down, right from left, forward from backward?

It gave him pause.

Nevertheless, like many men and women before him, he gritted his teeth and knew the bravery of the lost, the disenfranchised. Formerly pluckless, Jake now, for the first time, knew bravery.

Jake took one step off his doorsill.

Jake did not fall. He did not plummet into the abyss.

The void held him up, yet there was a sensation of being part of the void that was unnerving. He took a few more tentative steps. He was moving outward.

Suddenly dread rose in his throat like vomitus. He spun around. His home was still there. It looked like a cardboard cutout against the vacant background. Could it be possible that Jake's house was the only bona fide thing left in the universe? Or, another hypothesis occurred to Jake: perhaps everyone woke up this morning to find him or herself alone, seemingly the only tangible point in immobile space.

The universe was rife with anxious explorers walking into the unknown!

Jake took another step, and then another.

JAMES ROYCE

In the 1960s James Royce lived in a suburban enclave tacked onto the side of Memphis, Tennessee. It was called Raleigh and it was new and shiny with gravel roads and houses or the frames of houses, every hundred yards, and the abundant trees were leafy and full of life. Raleigh was being born. James Royce was ten or eleven. He was small and pale and his white hair disappeared in the sun and made James look like an angel with a head made of eggshell.

James Royce didn't think he fit into the world. He felt this way even when he was a toddler. Things other kids did with ease and grace came hard to him. His street, Kenneth Street, was populated by young families, and there were many children his age. They did things so effortlessly. They threw balls and caught them. They kicked and fought and spit and cussed. James liked them immensely. They all rode bikes, and James Royce did not know how. His balance, his fear of falling and his fear of failing tied James up in knots and rendered the simple human machinery required to balance upon and move a two-wheeler far beyond his abilities. It made him ill to try.

Linny Thayer lived across the street from James. She was tall and blonde and tomboyish. She was James Royce's best friend. He loved Linny. Not like a girlfriend, though there were mysterious stirrings in him sometimes when Linny was near. Once she left the bathroom door open and said to James, "You can watch me pee if you like." James was spellbound. Her soft shorts and white panties were pooled at her feet. Her legs shone like brilliant playthings. And she sat there smiling at James Royce and James felt less lonely. He fit in somewhere, he thought. He fit in with Linny.

James used to play Barbies with Linny. She had this elaborate pink and pale blue plastic house and car, also other dolls related to Barbie, a sister doll and a boyfriend doll. Linny told James to pretend to be the boyfriend. His name was Ken. Once walking to Linny's house with one of the dolls in his hand a car slowed down next to James. It was full of older boys. They pointed and laughed. James begged his face not to cry but his face didn't listen. Tears came. His neck and throat felt hot.

Linny's family moved away after Linny's mother died of cancer. Linny's mother was Mrs. Royce's best friend. When she died James' mother stayed in her bedroom for what seemed an awfully long time. James worried the whole while. He thought something had gone wrong with his mother, like maybe her chemistry was upset. Perhaps she would catch the cancer that killed Mrs. Thayer and then she would be gone and James would be more alone, without a best friend and without a mother.

After three days, James' mother emerged from her room unexpectedly and the day was sunny and the air seemed scrubbed clean and clear. James' mother put her hand on James' head and leaned over and kissed him on his crown. She asked James if he wanted homemade waffles. This was James' favorite food and he never got to have it in the middle of the day. James knew then that his mother was back and that she would not die.

After he ate the waffles James went outside where everything seemed still and quiet. James walked his neighborhood as if he had been granted possession of it all. The street was freshly paved and there were black bubbles of tar which some of James' friends would pull out of the glistening roadway and chew as if they were licorice. The Thayers' old house now with a For Sale sign in the front yard, the spooky split level where the mean football coach lived, the fire hydrant that sat in front of the fireman's house, the one the fireman drove over sometimes returning home late and drunk: It was all saluting James Royce. At the end of his street, right before his street, Kenneth Street, intersected with another street, Joslyn Avenue, there lived a family of older twin boys and a sister who was as pretty as a TV star. James knew their names. Their last name was Appling. There was something mysterious about them that captured the imaginations of James and the other youngsters.

One of the boys was named Peck. That was his first name. He was seen outside more than his siblings, who tended to stay inside their two-story home. The house was as big as a palace to James. It was said that the Appling children read books and were very smart. The beautiful sister read books, it was said, that some of James Royce's teachers wouldn't understand. James loved this family, the Applings. Once Peck spoke to James on the school bus. The school bus usually frightened James because the driver was a rough farmer named Cow John, or that's what the kids called him, and because there were rough boys on the bus who did not live on James' street. Peck said, "Nice shirt," about a paisley shirt James was wearing. That was a good day.

James sat on the curb at the bottom of the Appling's driveway. Maybe Peck would appear and talk to him. Maybe the sister—Stella—would make a rare trip outdoors and James could ask her what she was reading. He had prepared that question in case he ever found himself alone in her presence. *What are you reading?*

James watched a stream of ants moving into a crack in the curb. They were so small and there were so many of them and James wondered if their world was as complicated as his, wondered if there were too many ants living underneath the curb and there were some ants undone by this. James had to stop himself thinking about the crowded, airless, underground ant home.

James heard a car slowing down on the fresh blacktop and he looked up. The car moved as if he were dreaming it. Inside the car was a driver, a man who must have been 25 or more, and beside him a scrawny boy with ugly teeth, sitting on the passenger side. James began to smile as they slowed. It was a beautiful day. His mother did not have cancer.

The boy on the passenger side sneered deliberately and made a gesture that James knew was ugly. He held up the middle finger of his hand. Then the car increased speed and was gone.

James sat still, afraid if he moved he would shatter. The world seemed to spin around him as if he were inside a clothes dryer. James mouth felt funny and his tears began to well. He couldn't speak or move for a moment. Why did that boy and that grown-up man hate James? He asked himself that. Why did they hate James Royce?

After a while James stood and listlessly walked home. His stomach was full of waffles and suddenly James hated waffles. They made him sick. He never wanted to have waffles again, or friends like Linny who disappeared, or dolls, or games to play, or tar bubbles to chew. He would never ride that bus again with that awful Cow John and he would not return to school. Maybe there were some friends who would wonder where he went but he wouldn't care. Maybe some people would be thinking about him as his absence lengthened. He would be a ghost to them. James Royce, that day, gave up on the world.

AS A CHILD

As a child I was wispy. I was made of balsa wood and gypsum. I could not run fast or kick a ball. I was other. The rougher boys told me to hate myself and my body. I found them repulsive, like a disease of the skin, yet I believed their assessment of me. Once, in horrible and shameful desperation, I tried to make them like me. I ached to be part of their easy camaraderie. I envied their swaggers, their very ugliness. There was another boy. He was like me, unathletic and peculiar, but worse, he was also an unattractive weed. He wore his greasy hair parted sharply on one side, and his glasses were thick like the glasses of old men. I forget his name. The rougher boys were merciless to him. So I endeavored to join in. For one brief, misguided moment, I decided to be the bully instead of the bullied. I spat out, with impatience and ignoble heat, louder than I intended, "He wears pink underwear!" I don't know why I came up with this particular witty construction. And the pack of toughs looked at me as if a clod of earth had found voice. And then the worst of the rough boys, the one with a pinched rodent's face, hawked back at me, quick like a slap, "How do you know?" And they all laughed and spit and banged away, their doggish cackling echoing down the long polished school hall. The other boy and I looked at each other. There was pain in his eyes. He looked at me the way one looks at a pet that has to be put down. He pitied me. And I wanted to run after him and express my blistering regret. I wanted to tell him that I didn't belong in their vile crew, that I was more like him. But, of course, I didn't. I couldn't. I was not made for such compunction. So, today, almost five decades later, I still have this foulness within. It corrodes like undercooked food. It feels like a growth, a child growing inside me. The child is puckered and hideous and bred from darkness. He is mine. I hold him and, at night, I call him by many names. I call him my own name and I call him the names the monsters invented, long ago, in the baneful rooms of their exile, from which they are still emerging, day by forlorn day.

How to Be a Man

"And how does it feel to go down into the water with your eyes wide open, and your mouth gaping, so that you can see and taste every inch of the descent?"
—Peter Ackroyd

Waiting in his therapist's office, Rodney Carp was reading a women's magazine, an article about a man who built an entire home underwater. Because Rodney had lived his life with the name Carp and taken a bloody bruising for it, he was fascinated by all things aquatic.

It reminded him of a childhood storybook called *The Fishman Nicolao*; it was about a man who could live both on land and underwater. It was Rodney's favorite book. He was a reader; he lived in books. This was at a time in human history—the mid-1960s—when it was important that a growing boy be only one thing: tough. Rodney was not tough. He could not catch a ball and he could not run fast. He dreamed about living underwater like Nicolao because he imagined there he would be free of bullies.

His mother, mousy and slight, a grin like a cringe, was indulgent. Rodney's father was stoic, like his entire generation, until he grew exasperated with his only child.

"Put the goddamn books down and go outside. The boys are playing corkball. Why don't you join?"

A shudder went through Rodney's slight frame.

One day his father came home wearing a self-satisfied smirk. "You wanna read?" he said. "Read this."

And he threw down in front of Rodney a small pamphlet entitled, "How to be a Man."

Rodney's heart sank. His father would never love him.

And here Rodney was, 34 years later, in his therapist's office, prepared to talk about the dreams he was having about his now-deceased father.

"Whatcha readin?" A voice like a mermaid's.

Rodney looked up from the depths of fancy. It was that receptionist, Clark, with her nails like talons and her hair pulled back so tightly her face seemed inflated.

"Women's Day?" Clark tittered.

Rodney flushed royally.

"Article on—" but he stopped. Why explain?

"How were your dreams this week?" Dr. Moscoe asked, once Rodney had settled onto the settee and made himself receptive to transformation.

"Same," Rodney said.

"Underwater?" Dr. M asked.

Rodney nodded. "Dad dead."

"Been out any? Did you tell me you were going to start going out evenings?"

"No."

"I believe you did promise that, Rodney."

"I meant yes, I promised. And no, I didn't. Go out."

"What about—the woman, the girl, you went to school with, the one you ran into at the supermarket?"

"Candy."

"Yes. You told me you had a nice chat. Perhaps you could look her up."

"I told her I liked her dress. It wasn't much of a chat."

"Still, before next time ..."

After his session Rodney went home. Rodney worked from home as a remote designer for one of the major electronics companies. He spent his time in front of a computer. Tonight, as the screen whirled into view, he walked away. He opened the pull-down staircase to the attic and climbed the rickety ladder into the depressing fusc of his collected past. He thought he might find his old high-school annual and look up Candy's picture. Maybe he would call her.

He brought down a box marked "Childhood—Teen Years." He emptied it onto his dining room table. It was a horrible agglomeration. The detritus of a life lived indoors, a life apart. Old report cards, snapshots, pieces of toys, which, it can only be assumed, once gave joy.

And there, lying atop the ruins, like a fish floating in an aquarium, the damned pamphlet: "How to Be a Man." It was yellowed and foxed and gave off an odor like a sour tarn.

Rodney opened it as if it were bad news from afar. The words swam upward. They were unfamiliar. Had he ever read it? Had he ever pleased his father? He could not remember. The page he turned to was headed: *Are you a man or a fish?* Surely, he was hallucinating. His history was contaminating the pool of his rational mind.

The more he stared the more it hypnotized him. The print began to spin like a maelstrom, dizzying Rodney. A vision erupted in his corrupted noodle: a man swirling down a drain, a deadly eddy. The booklet slipped from his hands. He *was* spinning, traveling. He was leaving the earthbound world. "This is it," Rodney thought. "Now I leave my life behind."

"This is how the great Nicolao was transformed." The very earth under Rodney's feet gave way. It was a sinkhole, a gateway to the pelagic depths. *Goodbye*, Rodney said. *Goodbye, world*, as he moved downward until there was no up and down, no direction. There was only this watery place, this atmosphere of airless serenity, his abundance, his hadal hideaway, his new home.

ACKNOWLEDGEMENTS

Some of the stories in *As a Child* have previously appeared in literary journals, as follows:

"Pilkie Invents a Word" in *Punchnel's*
"A Very Short Story About a Hired Gun" in *14 4 30*
"Dante Gator" in *Battered Suitcase*
"Two Doors" in *Pure Slush*
"A Man and a Man/A Man and a Woman" in *Double Shiny*
"Something about Clea" in *Punchnel's*
"Cracker Hobgoblin" in *Twaddle*
"More Specific Horoscopes" in *Anomalous Press*
"Noctambulation" in *Ten Thousand Monkeys*
"God and the Devil: The Exit Interview" in *Grey Sparrow*
"Big House" in *Marco Polo*
"Slim Harpo Blues" in *Blue Crow Magazine*
"Tropic of Bernard" in *raccoon*
"Viator" in *Press 1*
"Chip" in *Grey Sparrow*
"The Travels of Cocoa Poem Lorry" in *Free State Review*
"Alan's Approach" in *Strawberry Press*

"Blunge" in *Muse Apprentice Guild*
"The History of Lungfish Melody" in *Juked*
"Rock Paste" in *Cezanne's Carrot* and Dzanc Press's *The Best of the Web 2009*
"Luda Christ" in *Heavy Glow*
"Bucky Bustard" in *Punchnel's*
"The Reviewer, the Author" in *Monkeybicycle*
"Living with Anderson" in *JMWW*
"He's Gone" in *Ping Pong*
"The Only One-Armed Man I Ever Knew" in *Verbsap*
"A Walk in the Woods" in *Thieves Jargon*
"The Voice and Me" in *Salt River Review*
"As a Child" in *Grey Sparrow*
"The World Went Away" in *Contrary*
"James Royce" in *Germ Magazine*
"How to be a Man" in *Esquire/Narrative4*

OTHER BOOKS BY COREY MESLER

POETRY

For Toby, Everything for Toby (1997) Wing & The Wheel Press
Ten Poets (1999) editor, only Wing & The Wheel Press
Piecework (2000) Wing & The Wheel Press
Chin-Chin in Eden (2003) Still Waters Press
Dark on Purpose (2004) Little Poem Press
The Hole in Sleep (2006) Wood Works Press
The Agoraphobe's Pandiculations (2006) Little Poem Press
The Lita Conversation (2006) Southern Hum
The Chloe Poems (2007) Maverick Duck Press
Some Identity Problems (2007) Foothills Publishing
Pictures from Lang and Fellini (2007) Sheltering Pines Press
Grit (2008) Amsterdam Press
The Tense Past (2010) Flutter Press
Before the Great Troubling (2011) Unbound Content
Mitmensch (2011) Folded Word Press
The Heart is Open (2011) Right Hand Pointing
To Writing You (2012) Origami Poems Project

Our Locust Years (2013) Unbound Content
My Father is Still Dying (2013) Flutter Press
Body (2013) Chapbook Journal
The Catastrophe of my Personality (2014) Blue Hour Press
The Sky Needs More Work (2014) Upper Rubber Boot Books
The Medicament Predicament (2014) Redneck Press

PROSE

Talk: A Novel in Dialogue (2002) Livingston Press
We Are Billion-Year-Old Carbon (2005) Livingston Press
Short Story and Other Short Stories (2006) Parallel Press
Following Richard Brautigan (chapbook) (2006) Plan B Press
Publisher (2007) Writers Write Journal Press
Listen: 29 Short Conversations (2009) Brown Paper Press
The Ballad of the Two Tom Mores (2010) Bronx River Press
Following Richard Brautigan (full-length novel) (2010) Livingston
    Press
Notes toward the Story and Other Stories (2011) Aqueous Books
Gardner Remembers (2011) Pocketful of Scoundrel
I'll Give You Something to Cry About (2011) Queen's Ferry Press
Frank Comma and the Time-Slip (2012) Wapshott Press
The Travels of Cocoa Poem Lorry (2013) Leaf Garden Press
Diddy-Wah-Diddy: A Beale Street Suite (2013) Ampersand Press

COREY MESLER has published in numerous journals and anthologies. He has published eight novels, five full-length poetry collections, and three books of short stories. He has also published a dozen chapbooks of both poetry and prose. He has been nominated for the Pushcart Prize numerous times, and two of his poems were chosen for Garrison Keillor's Writer's Almanac. His fiction has received praise from John Grisham, Robert Olen Butler, Lee Smith, Frederick Barthelme, Greil Marcus, among others. With his wife, he runs Burke's Book Store in Memphis, Tennessee. He can be found at CoreyMesler.wordpress.com.

www.ingramcontent.com/pod-product-compliance
Lightning Source LLC
Chambersburg PA
CBHW030824020726
47499CB00006B/2055